SHARED NIGHTMARES

Edited by

STEVEN DIAMOND & NATHAN SHUMATE

Published by
Cold Fusion Media
http://www.coldfusionmedia.us

COLD FUSION
MEDIA

Cover illustration "For In Dreams We Weep" by Dan Verkys,
http://www.gardenofbadthings.com
Model Silvia Alessandrini

Published at Smashwords by Cold Fusion Media
http://www.coldfusionmedia.us

CONTENTS

INTRODUCTION

People ask me why I like horror so much, and why I've always been a fan. The truth is, I haven't always thought the world of horror. I never read it. Didn't care. But then I read Brian Lumley, F. Paul Wilson, Robert McCammon, Sarah Pinborough and Joe Lansdale. Everything I thought of horror changed. It wasn't the blood and guts freakshow that I'd been led to believe it was.

What I've come to understand is that horror is about preying on the primal fears of humanity. Often times it's what *isn't* seen that has the greatest impact. Sometimes it's personal, sometimes it globe-spanning. Regardless, I started seeing horror in every other genre I read. Epic fantasy, science fiction, thrillers… everything. There was always some element of horror hiding inside, waiting to be uncovered.

In early 2014 I was watching a TV show—the funny thing is that I can't even remember which one—and there was a line that talked about people sharing dreams, and for some reason my brain said, "Yeah, but sharing *nightmares* would be way more interesting." I pitched the idea of an anthology to Nathan Shumate because I loved how he'd edited my story in *SPACE ELDRITCH II*. He agreed without question—because he's awesome like that —and I started recruiting authors. I know a few. What shocked me was how readily these authors were willing to take time out of their insane schedules to write original fiction for this collection. Bestsellers, award nominees and winners… I kind of expected a lot more rejection.

For the authors in this collection, these wonderful individuals who said yes and then didn't back-track, I'm eternally grateful. I'm still learning this whole editing thing, and each and every one of these authors backed me up the whole way.

Thank you.

So, here we are. Twelve stories. Horror in one way or another, all centered around dreams and nightmares. What more can I say?

Sweet dreams.

Steven Diamond
October 2015

FATHER'S DAY

Larry Correia

"I won't let you kill my daughter."

The Program woman gave me a patronizing smile. She was used to dealing with parents like me by now. "Now, Mr. Brody, I can understand your concerns, but it isn't like that at all. She will be perfectly safe. In fact, she'll be well cared for in one of our finest medical establishments."

"Uh huh…" I pretended to study the paperwork she expected me to sign, and then I glanced around the tidy government office. There were posters on the walls about doing our civic duty to help defeat the Dreaker menace, warnings about sleeping only during the mandated times, and even cartoons for the kids about the importance of taking their issued sleeping pills. The Program woman watched me with her cloying fake sympathy the whole time. A robotic security guard was standing directly behind my chair. That made sense. Some parents were bound to react violently when given the news that their child was being drafted to fight in the Dream War.

She must have gotten tired of waiting for me to sign, so she tried again. "We instituted mandatory blood testing for specifically this reason. There are so few people who can do what she can. She has a wonderful but rare gift. Maximizing that gift will benefit not only the city of Baltimore, but the entire human race. She's a very lucky girl. A very special girl."

I didn't like how this know-it-all bitch kept referring to my daughter. "*She* has a name."

"Of course!" But then the Program woman froze when she couldn't immediately recall what it was. My child was just another asset to these people to use up and throw away. Trying to play it cool, she glanced down at her data pad. "Wendy... And Wendy will be very happy living in the Safe Zone."

"You're going to make her into a vegetable."

"Somastasis is nothing like that," she lied right to my face. No compunction, no hesitation, just the party line.

"What is it, then?"

"When the invasion began, Dreamers were the only reason mankind survived at all. Less than one percent of the surviving human population has the genetic capability to fight off a Dreaker attack during REM sleep. On their own, a Dreamer can only protect a small area, and only for short periods of time. The Public Safety Program developed somastasis so that special individuals—like your daughter—could share their gift with the whole community."

"You didn't answer my question. I know damn good and well what somastasis does. It's a medically induced coma. You can lie all you want, but everyone knows what really happens."

She frowned. "I don't know about—"

"It's a medically induced coma, because sleeping all night isn't enough for you. Oh no, once you figured out how the Dreamers worked, you put them on drugs and forced them to sleep ten, fifteen, even twenty hours a day. For the public good, you said, but that still wasn't enough for you parasites. You need them to fight twenty-four seven, and you don't give a shit about what it does to them."

From the look on her face, I was beginning to get on her nerves. "It's a sacrifice for the good of mankind."

"The Dreamers already go to battle for the rest of us every single night. Every time that sweet little girl lays down her head, for her whole entire life, a thousand monsters have lined up to take a shot at her. Horrors you can't even imagine, but she fights the Dreakers so we don't have to. You don't know what that's like, doing that every single night, and you think that's still not fucking good enough?"

There was a vibration of an electric motor and one hard metal hand was placed on my shoulder.

"Stand down, Ajax," she told the robot before it ground my bones into powder. "There's no reason for profanity, Mr. Brody. If you become upset, I'll have security escort you from the premises."

Of course I was *upset*. Only a soulless bureaucrat could expect a father to respect bullshit protocols more than their own child.

"I understand your anxiety, I truly do, and I empathize with it." She'd probably been told to say that to angry parents during some sensitivity training. "Perhaps I failed mention that the families of our volunteers are extremely well compensated. Your loved ones will be provided housing in the Safe Zone and given a generous living stipend."

Like a bribe could replace a kid. "Fuck your money," I snarled. The robot squeezed my shoulder to remind me that it was *illegal* to be impolite to government employees. "You're condemning Wendy to hell."

The Program woman tapped her fingers on her desk, probably flagging me as a subversive in their system. "This is a public safety issue, Mr. Brody. If you don't sign those papers, we will be forced to take legal action."

I would have stood up and stormed out, but I was being held down by a robot.

"It will take a week or two for the orders to be processed through Public Safety. I suggest you reconsider during that time." The Program woman leaned forward conspiratorially, as if our entire conversation wasn't being recorded. "Look. You seem like a loving father, Mr. Brody, so I'm going to level with you. This is a national crisis. Frankly, the Dreakers are winning. A third of the country is lost, and we're doing better than the rest of the world. We *need* your daughter, and one way or the other, she's going in the Program. The Dreamers are our only hope."

Wendy had just turned six.

I had nightmares that night, but so did everyone else in the world.

The Dreakers were masters at understanding whatever was troubling you, and then they'd dredge up every ugly bit in your subconscious and turn it against you to chip off little bits of your sanity. It was like having a loose tooth that you just kept poking at with your tongue, wiggling it until it popped out.

So when the aliens invaded my mind that night, it was all images of

Wendy being ripped away from me, of her brothers and sisters crying, of the lab-coated Program officers sawing open her skull and shoving electrodes into her brain. Of me letting it happen.

The Dreakers were persistent alien bastards. We didn't know where they came from. I couldn't understand the science of it, but they didn't exist in the same dimension as we did, so we couldn't see them, and no one could figure out how to communicate with them. We didn't even know what they wanted or what had brought them to Earth to begin with. One day the nightmares began, and the world started falling apart. All we really knew about the Dreakers was that they'd invaded the dreams of everyone on Earth, and so far, they'd managed to kill about half of us.

"I miss Mommy," Wendy said out of nowhere.

"Me too." It was morning and I was cooking our breakfast of powdered eggs and SPAM. There'd been no food shipments into our zone this week, so we were living off what we'd managed to store. The electricity was out again, but at least the gas lines still worked.

"I'm sorry I couldn't save her."

"It's not your fault, honey."

Wendy didn't sound sad, just matter-of-fact. "I didn't sleep good that night so I couldn't keep the monsters away. They got in Mommy's head and broke everything. They made her too scared to live. That's why she took all the pills."

My eyes had gotten watery. "Don't talk about it. You're good."

"No. I'm not."

"Don't say that." I brought her the plate of eggy mush. She was wearing her favorite princess dress. I'd traded for it years ago, and it was falling apart, and she'd outgrown it, but Wendy wouldn't part with. She said it made her feel pretty. "Mommy always said you were a superhero."

"Kinda, but I'm not all the way."

Her older brother had found a box of crayons in the street when he'd been scavenging yesterday, and Wendy was drawing a picture. She set the old piece of scrap paper aside to eat. Her drawing was a bunch of green and black squiggles. "What's that?"

"One of the monsters. His name is... Well, it's a funny name, with a lot of 's' sounds in it," she said proudly. "*Sissassack.* But I can't say it right. He's the one that was inside Mr. Nelson's head when he shot everybody."

They hadn't bothered to reopen her school since the massacre. I picked up the paper and tried to decipher the picture. It was either too alien, or she was just as bad an artist as I was. "Why don't you draw something happy?"

"This is happy, Daddy." She looked up and beamed at me with her gap-toothed grin. "I found Sissassack last night and made sure he'll never hurt anybody again."

I sat down across from her. "How'd you do that?"

Wendy took the red crayon in her fist and violently scribbled all over the picture.

The bastards cut off food rations to the entire zone. It was a warning that the government that had the power to give everything also had the power to take it all away... But I still wouldn't sign their damned papers.

"What're we going to do, Dad?" my oldest son asked when he relieved me from guard duty. The two of us were on the roof, watching the barricades. The further you got from the Safe Zones, the more the city turned to shit. To conserve the Dreamers we were all ordered to sleep at the same time. That was easy for the government to declare, since they weren't out here dealing with gangs, looters, or people the Dreakers had possessed.

"I'll trade for food."

"What've we got to trade? And with who?"

"I don't know." He was too young to really understand what a father was willing to do to provide for his children. "I'll think of something."

"We could go west. They couldn't take Wendy from us there. There's no government at all on the west side."

I shook my head. That side of Baltimore was controlled by warlords. Once they figured out that Wendy was a Dreamer, they'd kidnap her just as fast as the Program. "That's not a good idea."

He was scared and trying not to show it. When I was his age I was play-ing video games and getting up the courage to talk to girls, not trying to make sense of the apocalypse. "Then what're we going to do?"

"I'll think of something," I said again. "I promise."

* * *

The Program sent a "team" to retrieve Wendy, but it was actually more like an army. Their armored vehicles crashed through our barricades. Helicopters hovered over the block, searchlights playing back and forth across the mostly abandoned buildings. The neighbors had sold us out. Even though Wendy had been protecting their dreams all these years, they were scared and hungry, so they told the Program right where to find us.

My oldest daughter tried to talk to them. They shot her down in the street. I was too stunned to move. Then my boy reacted, running to his sister, and they gunned him down too.

Wendy was hiding behind my legs, screaming and crying. *Don't let them take me away, Daddy! Don't let them take me away!* I tried to fight. It was like my hands were too clumsy to work. Though I'd tested it, the pistol I'd traded for wouldn't fire. The trigger weighed a millions pounds and when I did get it to shoot, I couldn't hit anything. The Program soldiers just laughed as they dragged me away from Wendy and beat me mercilessly with their batons.

I couldn't do anything, and the clubs just kept falling, breaking bones and splitting skin. Wendy was begging for them to stop. I reached out for her, but a Public Safety Officer, faceless behind his riot helmet, had grabbed her by the hair and was dragging her away. She was kicking and screaming, but he picked her up and hurled her into the open back of the armored car, where she bounced off the walls and lay crumpled on the floor.

The faceless man slammed the hatch shut.

"Daddy?"

I woke up, covered in sweat and shaking. I could still see my other kids lying dead in the street. I could still feel the clubs. But I was lying in my own bed. Somebody had turned the lights on.

"Wake up, Daddy." Wendy was standing next to the bed. She put one tiny hand on my arm. "You were dreaming."

"I know. I'm okay now." I hugged her tight. What good was a father who couldn't protect his own family? "I won't let anything happen to you." That had been too real. It had been a long time since Wendy had let something that awful slip into our house. "Damned Dreakers," I muttered.

"It wasn't the monsters this time, Daddy."

I started to cry.

In the olden days before the invasion, they could have called on the phone, or sent an email, or even had a letter delivered. When I was young, every-body, even poor folks, had a cell phone. But now there was no phone service and no internet. Hell, we didn't even have reliable electricity. It had been five years since they'd disbanded the postal service, so when the Program wanted something, they had to come in person.

They hadn't attempted to cross the barricade. It had been the Washington family who had been guarding the block last night, and they'd seen a Pro-gram car stop at the entrance and toss the package over the gate. The fat en-velope had my name on it, but there had been plenty of warnings written on the package, so by the time I found out, the whole compound knew.

A judge had signed the papers for me. I had twenty-four hours to turn Wendy over to the Program, or we would be in violation. Anyone who har-bored us would be criminals.

They threatened to burn the entire block if they had to.

"I hate to say this, but we got no choice, Brody. You know what they'll do if we don't turn your girl over." Douglas was the nominal leader of our block and my best friend. I could tell that the others had already talked it over be-fore they'd fetched me. I already knew what they were going to say. "You helped build this place, and we're thankful for everything Wendy's done, but we voted…"

"After all that she's done for you, after all these years she's kept you safe, you'd just turn her out like that?" I had to ask, though I already knew the answer. Of course they would.

"You're the reason we ain't got no food deliveries," Colvin said. "Sorry, brother. They ain't leaving us no choice. My kids got to eat."

"So that's it? You survive one more shitty day, so you can cower through one more horrible night? What're you going to do without Wendy to keep away the Dreakers?"

"I don't know," Douglas said, spreading his hands apologetically. "I just don't know. We might get along without her, we might not, but we can't stand up against the Program. Aliens might screw with our heads later, but the Program boys will just shoot us now. We already took a vote. You and

13

your kids can stay if you want, but Wendy's got to go. I don't know why you'd want to stay, though. If the Program offered my family a spot in the Safe Zone, I'd take it."

"No possessed in there, that's for sure," Colvin agreed.

"You think it's so damned easy, you'd let them hurt one of your kids to save the rest? You chickenshits have no idea what that's like."

Douglas just shook his head sadly, then walked away. Most of the other adults followed him.

"He stuck up for you, but a vote's a vote." Colvin poked me in the chest. "You got twenty-four hours, Brody. Pack your shit, because you've got to go."

For the first time in six years, there were no nightmares at all.

I dreamed about my wife, before the Dreakers had broken her mind and spirit, back when she was kind-hearted and full of love. I dreamed about the world as it used to be, with hope and promise. I dreamed about friends and family now dead or missing, but in my dream they were all alive, and I dreamed of my children growing up in that idealized old world instead of the real one.

It was wonderful.

When I woke up, Wendy was waiting for me. She was wearing her princess dress and a backpack with cartoon characters on it. The pack was stuffed with clothing and her favorite toys. It was like a child's interpretation of what you'd need on an epic quest.

"I didn't have nightmares last night. Did you do that?"

"That was my present to you. I tried extra-hard to chase off the monsters 'cause today's Father's Day."

I hadn't looked at a calendar in a long time. "Thank you."

Wendy shrugged in that adorable way that only the truly innocent can. "I had to try hard to help just our house, so I let the monsters scare everybody else more than usual. Serves them right for being mean to you."

"What's with the backpack?"

"It's a long walk to the the Safe Zone."

"We can't go there, silly. They're going to—"

"Shush!" Wendy held up one finger and poked me in the lip. Her mother used to do the same thing. "I know what they'll do. I see their dreams like

I see yours, and they're going to put me to sleep forever."

I gently took her hand and moved it aside. "Which is why we can't go there." I didn't know where we were going to go yet, but we had to go some-where.

"You don't understand, Daddy. I don't mind. I see the dreams of the kids who are asleep all the time too. They were lonely, but they found each other. So they've made up their own world. On the light side is where all the peo-ple have gone. On the dark side is where the monsters come from." Wendy pointed around my bedroom. So grown up for such a little girl. "This is in the middle part. I'm going to the light so I can save the middle. It's very nice there. That's why I tried so hard so you could see it for yourself."

My dream?

"I didn't want you to feel sad for me. Mommy says it's time for you to let me go. I need to go be a superhero."

DREAMCATCHER

Sarah Hoyt

The man sitting across from me on the straight-backed chair facing my desk looked rumpled and sleepless. His short brown hair stood on end. The dark circles under his eyes had their own dark circles. His shirt was buttoned wrong.

He eyed me through half-closed lids. "You're not what I expected," he said.

"No," I said.

I'm not what anyone expects. Well, not anyone who has gone through counselors, psychologists, psychiatrists, priests, exorcists, group therapy, scream therapy, sleep therapy, antidepressants, depressants, and whatever else has been thrown at them before someone somewhere whispers my name and address or gives them my card.

They always come in looking like they're sure they got the wrong address and like I'm the wrong person. I'm too young at only 27, too female, too attractive. By which I mean I wear jeans and a nice blouse, my hair is blonde and well cut and I meet them in the sunlight, in a white carpeted office, with a glass desk and black, straight-backed leather chairs.

The only thing anyone unacquainted with my true vocation would think is odd about the décor of my office is the giant dreamcatcher behind my desk—a circular net of leather and feathers and beads. And that's not functional. Or at least if it is, I never learned how it worked. It's just decoration. A joke on the business name.

"It's a family business," I said. "Grandma did it. She taught it to me. So, it is what I do."

He hesitated. He didn't know what to do with his hands, and finally settled for resting them on his knees. He looked at my face, and then behind me, as though he were speaking intently to the spot in the middle of the leather dreamcatcher. It was ornamented with two red feathers and I found it really attractive myself, but I didn't think it warranted that kind of attention.

"It's the nightmares," he said.

"It usually is. When you're asleep?"

This brought his eyes back to me, with a startled glare. "When else?"

"Ah," I said. "You're lucky."

He frowned at my face, then sighed. His hand went up to massage the middle of his forehead, as though by that action he could release whatever demon troubled him. "Every night," he said. "Every night. It's like…" He lowered his hands, and made a vague gesture. "It's like I wake up from something horrible—No, like I just *did* something terrible, committed some horrible crime. I feel like I'll never again be clean, never again be innocent. It takes me a few minutes to realize nothing has happened, that I'm still in my bed. And then—" He looked back at the center of the dreamcatcher. "And then I fall asleep. And it happens again. I started by going to my doctor, who referred me to a psychologist. Who referred me to a psychiatrist. Who put me on various drugs, none of which helped me, and then he sent me to a priest. Father Buros at St. Helen's," he said. "He sent me to you."

"Ah. Yes. Father Buros." Father Buros was an old friend and had reason to know what I could do.

My potential client cleared his throat. "I'm not… I'm not of his flock. He was recommended as an exorcist, actually. But he said it wasn't his business, and… that you could help."

I edged towards the point to be made, the point that had to be made. Many of these people expected you to work for free. It went with the idea that I should be a single-toothed hag muttering my pronouncements over interesting-smelling fumes. "There is," I said, "the matter of pay."

He blinked at me, as though having trouble focusing—which he probably was, given his appearance. "Right. Father Buros said that you were expensive," he said. "But worth every penny."

"Well then," I said.

The man reached into the pocket of his pants, and brought out a check-book. He wrote rapidly, then handed me the check. "A retainer."

I looked at the check. Counted the zeros. Then I set it on my desk, face down. I'd noted the name. Mr. Ian Jones was a rich man, I guessed. Rich and desperate.

The room next to my office contained a sofa. I politely asked Mr. Jones if he needed to take anything to make himself sleep. He shook his head. He looked, to be fair, as though he were ready to drop.

I led him to the recliner behind a screen. "If you lie down here, I'll join you in a moment."

"Join me?" He looked at the recliner.

"Not on the recliner," I said primly. "In your dream."

"Oh," he said. He lay down on the sofa as though he were dropping into a deep sea. I guessed he'd be asleep in seconds.

My grandmother started teaching me the family business before I knew there was anything to learn. I never was sure if my parents knew what was going on.

She started when I was very young, telling me stories I only half-understood. Years later, when I'd gone to college, I realized what Grandma had told me were all the oldest myths. Roman and Greek, and earlier than that, stories of bulls splitting the world, of heifers giving birth to the vault of the sky and the multitude of stars.

In turn I told her stories of my dreams, and of that curious state between dream and waking when you feel as though you're able to enter the minds of those around you.

After listening to my stories, Grandma had become very serious and started telling me things I needed to know. Things I didn't even understand I needed to know.

The very first thing she taught me was a complex diamond shape, its corners ornamented with odd characters. She taught me to draw it on the floor, in chalk. She watched me doing it. She corrected me. "If you're ever threatened," she said, "no one can touch you if you stand in the middle of this symbol."

I had no idea how mere lines of chalk could protect me, or what I might need protection from. But I listened. I was three years old, and Grandma knew everything.

She drew it on the floor of my bedroom around my bed, and then she erased it, but told me the symbol remained, in spirit.

I didn't realize how much she worried about me, or what she worried about. I didn't think, then, that my dreams were anything special. Surely everyone was haunted by nameless terrors in their dreams. Surely everyone fought and fought, and woke up soaked in sweat and screaming.

"The important thing," my grandmother said once when she was baby-sitting me, "is to always make sure you know whose dream you're in." I was only six at the time, and my parents were out at Dad's company Christmas dinner.

"The second most important thing," she taught me later, "is to remember the path out of the dream." I was twelve and doing my school homework, and I nodded wisely, but didn't think about what she was saying. I didn't want to think about strange things, or anything beyond what I was taught in school. I liked things you could feel and touch, and dreams were danger-ous, slippery places.

"The third most important thing," Grandma said, as she entered my dream and beheaded the nameless horror that my high school boyfriend had turned into, "is to know how to take an ax with you into the dream, and how to keep it sharp." My boyfriend, Jordan, had become a tentacled, fanged creature following me through the labyrinths of sleep, trying to de-stroy me and devour everything I was. Grandma held up the dream ax, and it glinted sharp and dangerous, stained with the green ichor of the creature that Jordan had turned into. Somehow it didn't come as a shock to me, the next day, to hear he had died in his sleep. It wasn't until I was eighteen that everyone found out about the other girls he'd killed. Someone going through his belongings had found the souvenirs. Bits of bone. Scraps of hair.

"Grandma," I said. I'd driven across country from college, and now perched on her kitchen stool across the table from her, a plate of cookies and a pot of tea between us. "You really did come into that dream when I was fourteen, didn't you? You really did save me? From Jordan Ahlgreen?"

And my grandmother had talked to me in her homey kitchen, smelling of freshly baked oatmeal cookies, over cups of hot tea. "There are things—" She sighed as though trying to find words to express ideas that were older than words. "Being human is not as simple as it seems. We're not just physical creatures, going about our lives, day to day. It's not all food and flesh. That's just being monkeys. Clever monkeys, maybe, but monkeys.

"Being human is something far more complex. It's the accumulated memories, hopes, thoughts, and dreams of all those people who lived on the Earth before us. It's… stories. The things that weren't quite men in the dark of the cave remembered a time when they weren't flesh. Or perhaps people are right, and they dreamed up things to explain the clap of thunder, the flash of lightning, the seasons, the scouring ice and the scorching summer, the growth of plants, the miracle of animals. All those things they dreamed up stayed. All those things came to exist. Oh, in stories and in words passed on, sure, but in the dreams too. Dreams shaped by stories and dreams seeping into each generation's heads.

"In a way all those thoughts, all those ideas, all those images created a whole world. A world full of ideas and cunning and plans. A world that is as much part of humans as are hands and feet, and clever thinking brains." She looked intently at me. "A world that dreams of becoming *the* world. The only world humans live in. A world that wishes to break out into reality and rule the clever thinking brains. To prevent it, there are other things. Symbols and stories. And there are people." She nodded again and poured me a fresh cup of tea, somewhat stewed and dark amber, in the porcelain cup. "People like Jordan, who let themselves be taken over to do the bidding of the dark. And people like us."

"Like us?"

"I was afraid, you know, you'd be taken over. People like us, who move in dreams, who can see into other rooms, who can walk the dream world at will, are at risk. We always are. It's a shadow world of undefined rules. It's easy to get lost."

"That's why you taught me the protection symbol so young?" I said.

"Yes. I knew then there was a good chance you were going to be like me."

"Are my parents like me too?" I asked, wondering whether I'd been going through life blind, while my family fought dream-monsters.

"No. Don't tell them about it. It would only disturb them. There aren't many of us born, and most of us get lost. Taken by one of the dream horrors. Which is what happened to your boyfriend. I guess he didn't have anyone to protect him."

"But you said… about the ax."

"Yes, it's important to learn to take the ax into the dreams. You see, people like us? We guard the entrance of this world. The dark, scary creatures—the blood-soaked dreams of the thing that lived in our minds before we were human, filled with power by centuries of worship, tainted with crimes of those they've taken over—those would come through everyone's dreams and everyone's sleep. If there weren't people like us."

"What are we?" I asked.

"We guard the borders," Grandma said.

That had been the beginning of my training. Grandma had left, four years ago, for that great sea of dream from which no one wakes, but she'd left me trained.

Now, in the larger room, on the other side of the screen that sheltered Ian Jones' sleeping form, I drew the ancient symbol on the floor. Then I got Grandma's ax. I kept it very sharp.

I lay down inside the symbol, holding the ax.

Sleep washed over me like a wave. It was training. You learned to fall asleep on command. I belonged to the only guard for whom falling asleep on my post was a requirement.

I walked a foggy path inside.

A sound of scraping and running. A sound of running feet and suddenly Ian Jones was there, grabbing at my arm.

"Run," he said, and pulled me, at speed, up an increasingly rocky path.

Behind us something shuffled and snorted. It sounded like a million bulls. A look over my shoulder told me it was much, much worse. These were bulls that had existed when our ancestors had been much smaller—and the bulls were not real bulls, but bulls as they had imagined them, crea- tures they'd sculpted in stone and gold and to whom they'd given fire-filled bellies and sharp horns, both of which were used for human sacrifice.

Which explained the smell that came from the mass of stomping, snorting, sharp-horned things following us. It was the smell of old blood, the smell of burnt flesh, the smell of sin and death and human despair.

Still looking back, I ran right into something. It was metal, and hard.

I turned around, just barely keeping my feet. It was a gate, an elaborate metal gate like one finds sometimes at the entrance to old mansions.

It was closed not with a lock, but with a red strip of fabric sealed with wax, like an old letter. Ian was trying to tear the silk.

The stomping mass came closer, closer.

I grabbed Jason's hands. "No. Don't do that. That seal is your protection. This dream is a trap."

He looked at me with uncomprehending eyes. I pulled his hands away more forcefully. "Stop that."

"They will catch us!" he screamed, as I turned him around to face the horror bearing down on us.

But I had an ax. I lifted my ax glinting in the dream-light. The herd of bulls made of bronze and stone, the creatures of dread and nightmare, tried to stop. But it was too late.

I swung the ax. The bulls bellowed as one with a primal sound, and hundreds of bovine heads rolled at our feet, as a wave of old, fetid blood washed over us and washed us away.

It washed us into a high tower, scoured by winds. At the foot of it, the sea beat with a sound like the screams of all the sailors who'd ever drowned.

"What did you do?" Ian Jones asked, looking at me, his eyes wide.

"I kept you from breaking the seals. The seals are the protections between us and those creatures. If you break all seven seals, they take you over. They ride you into our world. How many have you broken? How many in the past, in other dreams?"

"Three," he said. "Maybe four."

I narrowed my eyes at him. "These dreams are traps. They're traps to make you open the gates into the world." I told him what Grandma had told me about the dream world, and the old, unspeakable imaginings of humanity. I told him about Jordan.

"You mean if I break all the seals, they'll come into the real world, in my mind? That I'll turn into some sort of mass murderer?"

I shook my head. Normally, yes. Normally, I'd found that people tormented by this sort of dream were people who had the same capacity I had. They were people who could walk in the dream world and who hadn't been taught to watch themselves. They were vulnerable ones, who could become the ride and the creature of nightmare.

Those killers that committed acts that humans looked at and said "that's not human" or "that wasn't done by any human being"—those almost certainly were *not* human. Or they weren't human any longer.

I had reason to believe when Jack the Ripper sent his letter to the police "from Hell," he had meant it literally. Or at least from a dimension that looked so much like Hell as to be indistinguishable.

Now the tower was shaking. It was an old tower, not very tall. It must be like the early, rude constructions our ancestors made on shores threatened by the sea and navigated by the very first sailors cleaving close to the shore.

In those towers, during storms, ancestral humans had huddled, and shivered, and shuddered, afraid the sea would engulf all land. From those towers, they'd thrown human sacrifices into the immeasurable, incalculable sea.

A tentacle came through window.

Ian stepped back from it. He was learning. But he wasn't learning fast enough.

"There's that window," he said, pointing behind me. "If we jump from it —" The other window, away from the tentacles, had no signs or symbols, but only crossed bars over it, crossed bars set into primitive indentations in the stone.

"If we slide that aside—" he said.

"Will you not learn?" I asked. "Stand and fight."

I raised my ax and turned to the window. I cut the tentacle. And then another. And another. Ian had gotten a sword from somewhere.

"It was in the stone," he said. Which made sense, because dreams are like that.

He lurched forward. I stepped out of his way just in time. He speared a monstrous, dark eye that peered through the window.

The scream was deafening, like a million waves crashing into the shore at once.

And then the tower fell. And we were underground.

I didn't know where we were, but there didn't seem to be anything immedi-ately threatening us. The place we walked along was a rocky cavern. I had vague memories of being in a place that looked like this, when I was very young and my parents had taken me on a trip to Colorado and showed me all the abandoned and semi-abandoned gold and silver mines.

There was nothing scary about a mine *per se*, unless you were the sort of person who felt crazy claustrophobia when underground. I confess that basements aren't my favorite places, and that I'd prefer not to work in any underground facilities. But neither are they inherently terrifying on their own.

Ian and I walked side by side. He still had the large sword over his shoul-der. The strange thing was that, given the age of everything he'd seen in his dreams before—the primal bulls, the ancient tower— the sword was new, shining and golden. I would have expected a sword of the age that gave us legends of swords in stone: iron, crude, more suited to bludgeoning than to cutting.

It seemed out of place. It made me jumpy, even though the surroundings weren't immediately dangerous or threatening.

On second thought, mines *were* scary after all. People died underground, as the world collapsed on them.

I listened for the sounds of avalanche, for the distant knocks of tommy-knockers. I heard nothing. I should have felt better, but I didn't.

There was a prickling sensation at the back of my head, a sense that not all was as it seemed. I hefted the ax.

We were walking upward, walking in silence.

"Funny," Ian said. "I always thought that the person who took the sword from the stone was supposed to be king. Not just to kill monsters."

I murmured something. I didn't know what. The sense of wrongness twisted around me like a coil and made my skin prickle and my hair stand on end.

Up and up and up, in the secret dark, until we heard the sounds of water. Of course, I thought.

The river Styx. The great, unbreakable seal. The transition that could not be crossed back. The sign and symbol of all the barriers. The ultimate do-not-trespass to the daylight world.

Death and sleep are much the same thing, in old legends. Protecting from one and protecting from the other can become indistinguishable, connected.

There was a sound behind us now: Growling, slavering, scraping. The snapping of teeth.

I turned and looked into the eyes of Cerberus, all of its jaws snapping, while its four huge paws drew near.

And on the other side was the river Styx, dark and deep, the green sludge of eternity, the coldness of reality between us and the daylight world.

On the other side, the sun shone. On the other side, the birds sang. On the other side, my body lay stretched within chalk symbols that would keep me safe.

Before, in other nightmares, things had tried to eat me. Things had got so close that they tried to snap at me. But the symbols had kept me safe.

I didn't need to kill the horror coming closer and closer.

The river Styx gurgled just behind me, and on the shore, steps away, a boat stood moored with a cowled boatman waiting.

I could just walk there, get on the boat.

Ian had turned, and was lifting his sword.

Always know whose dream it is.

The sword glinted gold in the dream-light.

Cerberus suddenly tried to stop, propelled forward by his own momentum.

The mines looked like the mines I'd walked through as a child. No tommyknockers. No trapped miners. No ancient horrors.

And Ian was not like my other clients. He'd been trying to open seals, not simply to escape being devoured in his dreams. Not simply to escape being overtaken.

What kind of man takes a sword from a stone? A king. Where does he take a sword from a stone? In the kingdom he's claiming.

I was beyond Grandma's stories, but not beyond the legend. The king who comes from elsewhere, to rule all the land. The man who gets past Cerberus. Except Cerberus wasn't a monster in legend. Or rather, he was a monster but not an invading monster. He was a creature that reinforced the role of the Styx. He kept the dream creatures and the dead away from the daylight world.

There was only one thing I could do. It was a trap. This dream was a snare closing around me.

As Ian lifted his sword to behead Cerberus, I raised my ax and beheaded Ian.

I woke up, suddenly shaking, in half-light. The room next to my office was exactly as it should be. The clock on the wall, where I'd had it set so that I could see it first thing when I woke up, showed the dream had only taken five minutes.

I let go of the ax, which I'd been clutching so tightly that I expected the wood to be indented.

My mouth tasted foul and I felt like someone recovering from a fever, slow and muddled and not quite well.

I'd beheaded Ian. In the dream, I'd beheaded my client.

Such was my experience with this kind of thing that I thought two things at once: the first was how I was going to dispose of the body. And the second was whether his check would still clear.

I didn't doubt the dream had been a trap, meant not for him but for me. I wasn't sure how it could harm me, with me within a safe symbol. But I knew it could. Or perhaps not me, but the whole world. If Cerberus were killed, then the world would be left defenseless. Open to the invasion. Led by the creature who'd pulled the sword from the stone and claimed the kingship of the world of dreams.

A polite cough from behind the screen nearly made me jump out of my skin. I reached for the ax again. I stood.

Ian Jones stepped out from behind the screen. Despite only having slept a few objective minutes, he looked alert and rested. His eyes shone, and he smiled a little.

"Thank you," he said. "I have no idea what you did, but it worked."

He extended his hand to me, but I didn't take it. I stood in the middle of my drawn symbol, the ax in my hand.

He seemed puzzled, thrown off-balance by my unexpected rudeness. He bowed slightly. "Thank you," he said. And smiled broadly. "Worth every

27

penny. I... I'll see myself out."

I watched him walk through the door into my office, and then across the office, to my exterior door. I watched him let himself out to the outside world and close the door behind him.

I stood a long time before I stepped out of my protection and towards that same door. The office looked untouched. The door was closed.

It wasn't until I turned around that I saw the dreamcatcher had been ripped from top to bottom. I stared at it, a long time.

A symbol. Just a symbol. A symbol of my business.

I closed my eyes. I opened them again. The dreamcatcher was still torn.

I was awake. I was sure I was awake. And I'd done the right thing. I'd escaped the trap.

I replayed in my mind the arc of Ian's sword, the arc of my ax. Had he killed Cerberus before I killed him? Had the thing that crossed over, the thing that left my office, been the king of nightmares, finally let loose into the world after millennia, trailing behind him the nightmares from which no human would awake?

I looked out the window. Outside, nothing was visible but roiling fog. Odd weather for the middle of a summer afternoon.

I drew closer to the window, but still I could see nothing out there but fog coiling and twisting, tendrils of it winding around the window.

Fog, like formless dreams. Fog like those things that hide, half-thought, in the human mind.

Fog.

I trace the protective symbols again and again on the cold window glass.

Surely the sun will dispel the fog.

Surely the world is still there, sunny and clear and real. Surely, outside my window, past the banks of fog, the birds are singing.

Surely, the perimeter holds.

Surely.

It's very cold now, and the window is beaded with condensation. The symbols I drew become droplets that run and change into figures of nightmare.

INCUBATION

D.J. Butler

Will I be able to fall asleep now? What will I dream?

I look like hell.

That's me in the mirror over the pink chest of drawers with seafoam green accents, face pale but eyes dark, sweater filthy and torn.

It's Joan's sweater. It's tight on me.

My hands shake as I pick up the doll. Audrey's doll. I've just dressed it in its fanciest clothes, a red dress with sequins. I don't know what the doll needs sequins for, the damn thing is supposed to be a child, not some club-hopping tramp with her flat plastic cleavage all—

I'm sorry.

I hold the doll gently, cradle it. Shuffle into the hall and then the kitchen. The trailer is a double-wide, but that still means the kitchen is three steps away from Audrey's room. Double-wide just means there's room for Joan to have an office. And a place to.

To.

You don't know seafoam green from lime, you a-hole. Joan taught you that. You worthless sack.

I hear a choking sound, like someone's trying not to cry.

Joan will forgive me.

"I forgive you," I say. It comes out wrong. There's too much echo.

In the kitchen I stop for the bottle of Jack. I see my hand holding it, all the dirt under the fingernails. Even with the shovel, you get dirty when you dig a hole. When you.

I see *his* boots are still sitting inside the door. I thought I had gotten rid of them with. Had gotten rid of them.

So tired. So tired I'm getting stupid.

That's good. I need to sleep, so I can ask forgiveness. I've been trying, but I wasn't tired enough before. I'm pretty tired now.

The double-wide's floor creaks. Usually that's the sound of footsteps, and I jerk my head up. "Joan?"

Silence. "I'm sorry." But it's not enough.

I stumble out the back door. *He's* lying there, still, the bastard, I don't care. I can deal with *him* later. The moonlight is cold on my skin. It's a trick of the mind, maybe, I'm tired, but the light flickers. Can the moon do that? I don't think there are clouds, but I'm afraid if I try to look up I'll fall over.

I'm tired. Good.

I almost trip over the shovel, and its blade cuts into my foot. I'm too tired to curse, but it means I've arrived.

There's a patch of earth on the left, and shoved into it side-first is Joan's laptop. She's written papers on that computer, and novels and poems, so I guess it must have some of her soul in it. Also, she wrote e-mails to *him*.

"Bitch!" I spit.

The moonlight gets colder. I drop Audrey's doll.

"Sorry."

What's the doll's name? Melanie, maybe? Margaret? Madeleine? I try to bend at the knees to pick the doll up, and instead I fall forward and crash to the dirt. It's cold, and moist. I don't remember it raining, since. I scrabble around to get back onto all fours, and some parts of the earth sink deeper than others. Because under some parts of the earth. Under some.

I hear the sound of crying again.

I brush Madeleine off, but I only make her dirtier. I put her on the. On the bare earth.

Where did that bottle of Jack go?

I find it, and take a long drink. Maybe I should pour out some of the whiskey? But that's voodoo, giving liquor to the dead.

I don't want to do voodoo.

I can do this. I know what to do, Joan talked about this. There's a word for it, it's a chicken word. I don't remember the word, but that doesn't mean I don't know what to do.

I need to dream. I need to sleep, so I can dream, so I can ask forgiveness.

I've tried. Twice. Three times? Since I. Since I.

Since I found *his* boots, and then.

But I haven't been tired enough. I haven't been able to sleep.

Now I think I'm tired. And to be sure, I gulp all the Jack in the bottle.

That's... I don't know how much it is. Maybe two tumblers. It should burn as it goes down, but it doesn't. I don't even notice it.

This is what you do. You sleep in a special place, and the gods come talk to you in your dreams. The Greeks did it. The gods give you omens, they tell you your future, they bring you judgment and rest. Solomon did it, that's what Joan said, I don't read the Bible, the Bible's got nothing in it for me. She did all the reading, anyway.

"Didn't make you happy, did it, you filthy whore?"

I belch.

That's not right. That's no way to approach the goddess. I mean the dead.

"But you thought you were a goddess, didn't you?"

I pound the earth, I punch the laptop. I hurt my own fist.

I hear feet, I know they're feet, kicking up the dry, curled leaves under the gambol oaks. I punch some more.

I wish *he* wasn't there at my back, watching.

Someone's crying. I'm so tired.

I'm curled up like one of the leaves, in the dirt, but sleep doesn't come. Sleep doesn't come.

Sleep doesn't.

"Hello, Daddy."

I open my eyes. Audrey's standing there.

She's wearing her red dress with sequins. That isn't right, Audrey never had a dress with sequins. It's Audrey, though. She still has the gash across her throat where. The bleeding has stopped. I think I can see the white bones of her spinal column through the open wound. The wound that.

She just came out of her room at the wrong moment. If only she had been a sounder sleeper. If only Audrey. If only I.

"I'm sorry." The words come easy, I've been saying them for days. Ever since.

She says nothing.

"I'm very sorry."

She looks at me. Her eyes are full of moonlight, and cold. She stares down at me from the top of Mt. Nebo even though I know she isn't four feet tall and says nothing.

"It was an accident."

"Liar."

She is cold as the statue of St. Francis downtown, her lips barely move.

"But I didn't mean it." Someone's crying. "I didn't want to. I wasn't trying to."

"Everything you were," she says. Her voice is deep, wrong. "Every action, every word, every thought. Every single day. It could only end here. Here is where it started. We were here all the time."

In the dirt, my hand closes around something hard. I'm not looking for it, but I know what it is. Without trying, I pick up the.

"Now you must make it right."

Someone is crying.

"Tell me how," I say. This is what I came for.

"Make it right." These words come from behind me. They sound like the same voice, but I know the words are someone else's. Joan's.

Her laptop is gone.

I stand and turn. My feet sink into the dirt, which is wet, and sucks at my ankles. Nothing underneath, nothing in the soil, holds me up.

Joan stands in the yard. Behind her, the double-wide is on fire.

I don't remember setting the double-wide on fire.

Joan isn't alone. A man stands behind her. He has his arms around her neck, his face is in the shadow of hers so I can't see it.

"Him!" I shout.

He laughs.

"What I do is none of your concern," Joan says. I've heard these words before. Is she hugging *him*? She's not struggling, but her body twists and leaps around in *his* grip.

"Bitch!" I shout.

She looks at me in silence.

"I mean… he's hurting you!"

He doesn't stop. She doesn't stop *him*.

"You don't care. Don't pretend you care." Joan has gone all moon-eyes, too.

"I care." I do, I'm just. Broken.

"About me?"

"But what about...? It isn't right!"

"It never was right." Someone is crying. I think maybe it's Joan.

Maybe she doesn't want to be held by *him*.

"You were lonely," I say.

I almost say it was an accident, but I catch myself. "I'm sorry."

She struggles against *him*. *He's* choking her. The fire behind her burns tall and opaque.

I tighten my fist around the kitchen knife. It's the big one, the one you use to cut up carrots, the one I. The one I.

"I'm here to make it right!"

"So make it right," Joan says in that deep voice she shares with Audrey.

"Make it right," Audrey agrees.

I yell. I run at the man strangling Joan, and I feel the knife sink into his belly. There's a moment of resistance when the blade pushes against her sweater that's the only thing she was wearing when I found her in her office and against the muscles of her abdomen, and then it pushes right through. She falls, under the white fluorescent tube lights of the kitchen. She bangs hard into the counter once, and then falls to the linoleum. Shrieking.

No, Joan isn't shrieking. Joan is gone. I push her attacker away and he falls. No scream, just a sound like a sack of onions hitting the root cellar floor.

"Done!"

I turn to Joan and Audrey. They are tall white columns of marble above me, and the moon shines from their terrible, loveless faces. I drop the knife.

"I'm sorry," I say. "I told you I would make it right for you."

And then a terrible thing. They shake their heads, together.

No.

"This makes nothing right for us," they say. "It only makes it right for you."

I sweat and tremble. It isn't the Jack, it's the flames. Is it only the double-wide burning, or is the forest also on fire? "And for him," I say.

They only stare at me.

"It makes it right for him."

They grow taller, but say nothing.

I turn, my legs feel weak. I drop to the ground next to the man I've stabbed. His face is turned away from the fire, so I grab him by the hair and twist his head to bring his features into the light.

"It's me," I say.

I hear sobbing. Is it Audrey? Joan?

It isn't the man on the ground, the man with my face. He's still, dead.

I turn to Joan and Audrey, but they're gone. I don't see the doll, either, or the computer. Or the shovel, or the knife, or *him*. I see the flames arcing higher and higher into the night sky, and I feel cold.

And tired. So tired, and all I can do is wonder.

Will I be able to fall asleep now? What will I dream?

THE DEVIL ON MY SHOULDER

Tom Lloyd

I wish I had insomnia. It'd make everything so much easier. Sure, there are drawbacks, but there are drawbacks to everything.

I open my eyes and blink. There's a stack of cheap plastic bins stacked up in front of me and in my hand is a mop, the head wrapped in cellophane. For some reason I seem to have been contemplating buying it, though I've never mopped a floor in my life. I look up and there's an anxious Pakistani gentleman peering at me through the shop window, probably afraid that I'm about to do a runner and steal his mop. Do people do that? I mean, I know round here the thieves are mostly junkies, but would even they bother? It's a mop. The price tag says £5 but who'd even bother?

I've seen a few armed robberies in this area and our thieves are indeed the dumbest fucking animals you ever ran across. Half get seen off by staff and passers-by because they don't even know what to do with the weapons they brought. They can't afford baseball bats, let alone guns, so it's any piece of wood they picked up on the way, once even a plastic juggler's club. That guy got pole-axed by a sixty-year-old bundle of Jamaican rage with a hand-bag—still the best thing I've ever seen, before and after losing my virginity.

Okay, so the other half tends to fuck people up pretty badly because they *do* have the first clue about which end of the hammer you hit people with, but the dumb ones are a fun distraction for the devil on my shoulder so I try to keep a lookout for robberies.

I put the mop down and turn around. I think it's Tuesday, but it's one of those dull autumn days where you can't even tell if it's morning or afternoon. The rain's barely bothering to come down, it mostly seems to be hanging in the air so people walking under umbrellas still get it in the face. There's a Chinese restaurant across the road and the tables look empty so maybe it's early. I can smell something in the air, faintly sour and overripe, but the car fumes render it little more than a ghost scent.

The restaurant doesn't have a name, or rather doesn't have one I can read. There's just a white sign with some characters in black; shiny and new but apparently not wanting to encourage customers too much by having a name most can read. Having met a few landlords round here, I'm not surprised. Half the shops are just fronts, tax write-offs and somewhere to launder the off-the-books cash they get in.

I look down. At least I'm wearing shoes today. It doesn't matter if I'm asleep or awake; bare feet in a street where students puke and drop bottles most nights is never fun. Something niggles and I look harder. Those aren't my shoes. At least I don't think they are. I'm pretty sure, anyway. That doesn't mean I didn't buy them, I guess. They don't look new so I could have picked them up in a charity shop. Let's just say I don't remember buying them. That happens a lot.

In the window of the Chinese restaurant, a white-clad figure turns to face me. A hood which hides its eyes is pulled low over its face, halfway to a shroud, but I know it's looking at me all the same and I've seen that look before. It stays that way for a long while then turns and moves on, gliding as smooth as oil over the glass and on into the reflection on the next shop's window.

So that's one thing decided, I say to myself. *You nicked the shoes.*

"Stealing from a charity shop, Adam?" says a familiar mocking voice, right in my ear. "That's low."

"Fuck off," I mutter and start walking, first one way, then turning sharply as I realise I'm heading towards the local cluster of charity shops. I retrace my steps and instead head for an open green space just up ahead, abutted by an open-air café where they're more tolerant than most. I dig through my pockets and find some change. Maybe coffee will help.

"As sweet and black as sin itself," adds the voice laughingly. "Not the sin of stealing shitty shoes, of course, that's more of a latte crime. The pointless, barely-worthwhile crap of the coffee world."

I ignore it and in a few moments I'm past the row of shops, past their windows and reflections, so the voice is quietened again. It won't be for long, though I'll get a plastic spoon and sit as far from the chrome-sided Gaggia as I can, but any moment of peace is worthwhile. You live with this for long enough and you learn to pick your battles. The devil's a patient soul. It knows it'll win the war.

Given the drizzle, I've got the open part of the café to myself. Brown slat tables and chairs, amateur artworks inside and the pleasant babble of human voices in the distance. With the hood on my greatcoat pulled up, this really isn't so bad and though I know it won't last, it's about as close as I get to peace these days. I go through my pockets while I string the coffee out, an inventory of possessions. It's a habit I built years ago. When you don't know if you're awake or asleep, it's something for your brain to latch onto. And yeah, I know it makes me look crazy, this regular inspection of possessions, but I'm used to that. The accusation's hard to avoid anyway.

"Excuse me," intrudes a woman's voice. "Hello?"

I look up and manage to stare straight at the shiny plastic ID badge hanging on a lanyard around her neck. That's enough to make me flinch and jerk my head away, but not before I catch sight of an outline I know all too well, reflected in the plastic.

"Sorry, I didn't mean to startle you," she continues. "You just look familiar."

I force myself to ignore the reflection and meet the gaze of a forty-something woman holding an umbrella. There's a red silk scarf tied around her neck and I'm immediately reminded of Dracula. Then I realise I'm staring at her throat and mumble an apology. Even I know that tends to worry people, when the crazy people fixate on your jugular.

"Are you okay?"

I take a deep breath and gather my thoughts. I'm always pretty spaced when I wake, for want of a better word, somewhere I've no memory of going to. It takes a while before I remember how to be around people.

"I, ha, yeah. Fine. Weird day, that's all."

"Weird day," she echoes with a knowing look, like I just gave some sort of secret signal. She's early-forties with sandy, shoulder-length hair. Well-spoken too, one of the many good souls that work for charities round here. I blink and remember this is a charity-run café. I really might be familiar to her.

"I do know you," she says. "Andrew, is it?"

"Ah, almost. Adam."

"Adam, right. You came here to help out a few times—oh, it must have been a couple of years ago now."

Shit, I thought, sagging in my seat. I'm not exactly memorable normally; something must've happen to fix me in her memory and when it comes to stuff that happens to me, that's never good. "Sorry," I say pre-emptively.

"Sorry?"

I nod. "I don't remember, but I on some pretty heavy meds back then. I hurt anyone?"

She takes a small breath and pauses. I look up again and see it in her face. "You don't remember?" she asks quietly.

I shake my head. I would've tried to look pathetic and harmless if I knew how, but that's mostly how people see me anyway so she doesn't take a step back or call for the cops.

"Well," she begins, "I suppose you didn't start it."

We stay like that for a while, wrapped in an uncomfortable silence of my own making. A voice at the back of my mind, my own voice, reminds me I'd once have noticed she was attractive too. A little on the plump side maybe, but compared to all the stick-thin boyish students round here, that's a plus point. Medication's played havoc with my libido over the years, I honestly don't know if I'm so constantly horny I barely register attractive women any more, or whether I've just given up.

"Did I hurt anyone?" I ask meekly.

There's a faint cackle in the distance. I try not to twitch. The ID badge flashes round, offering me the glimpse of a reflection.

"*You fucked—,*" replies a distant whisper as it turns and turns back, "—*him up good.*"

She ignores the question, chooses not to give a reply that'll only make both of us more uncomfortable. "But you're doing better these days?"

I try not to laugh. "Better," I mumble. It might not be true but to the outside world I am and that's what matters. "The meds didn't let me think. Hard to work out what's real when you can't think straight."

"So you're off them now?" I can hear a clear note of disapproval in her voice. She must be pretty experienced in dealing with folk like me because to her I've now got 'paranoid schizophrenic' written all over my face and she's still more judgey than scared.

I shake my head and attempt a smile. "Something else. Amazing what you can get if you know the wrong people and sign any waiver they hand your way."

It's bullshit, but it's a line that's worked well over the years. Allude to experimental drugs you're happy to be a human test subject for and you can explain a lot while you ignore questions. I could come up with a real drug regimen easily enough, I've been on the fucking things since the age of five, but that's a tricky sell to people in the know.

"You're testing drugs?" she hisses. "That's outrageous! That's illegal, that's —"

"Better'n the alternative," I finish. "How long you reckon I'd live as a hallucinating zombie?"

"But you don't know the damage it could be doing to your body!"

I shrug the shrug of a man who can live with imagined side-effects. "Don't care, either. Alive for a while is better'n half-dead right up to the not-so-distant point you're really bloody dead."

Unexpectedly she sits at the table. That sends me into a bit of a jangle, I wasn't expecting that. Wasn't expecting to have this long a conversation all day, to be honest. I'm not homeless, I've got a tiny room in a doss house that's as precious to me as anything can be, but the other residents know some of my story. They're a decent bunch for hollow ex-junkies, broken ex-soldiers, tired ex-cons and all the other types of exes that slip through the cracks in this world.

Mental illness gets handed out along with your regulation shirts-two-pair, pants-two-pair, boots-one-pair package, but there are levels. Chronic depression, alcoholism or whatever are shitty things to go through and they scar you inside, but they don't automatically make you a write-off. Some people can deal with that; be knocked flat, bear the full weight of it all and get back on their feet again. Psychosis that no med in the world can even make a dent in, however? Folk get wary around that and as hard as you try, sometimes you just need to answer to the devil on your shoulder or it'll keep shouting so hard you can't hear the rest of the world burning around you.

"So do you have work?" she asks in a mother's tone of voice. It wakes something inside me even as I want to laugh at the idea, an ache I'd rather forget, but some scabs are only even paper-thin.

"Still not anything you'd call employable."

"So these experimental drugs don't quite do the job?"

"There's a devil on my shoulder still," I say in what I aim to be a light, cheerful tone of voice. Judging by her expression, I'm a bit rusty.

Almost on cue I feel a heavy hand descend upon my left shoulder and rest there. I don't look, I know it's not really there. The ID badge has turned my way and isn't moving now that she's settled in a seat. The white hooded figure is attempting to be fatherly, it seems, maybe inspired by the woman's concern, but as always I can see nothing of its face so the effect is more chilling than anything else.

"Do you want to come in out of the rain for a bit?" the woman asks. "There are biscuits for staff, in the back room. I could fetch you a couple. There are spare tables inside, you could dry out a bit."

I blink and look down. The weight on my shoulder lifts.

"No. Thanks, but I should probably be moving on."

When I look up the figure is still there, reflected in the ID badge, but it's turned away now. The world seems to shudder around me, the faint quake of earth emanating from my bones, but it's a minor one, just a modest aftershock.

"Sure?"

I glance over at the café building. It's a bright and welcoming place, so it's not really for me. "Too many windows and bits of metal. I don't like reflections much."

Despite the fact that I'm mumbling, she hears me and understands. Reflections are a trigger and I don't want her around to see that. Neither of us do. Out of nowhere I yawn, a great full-bodied yawn that takes control of every part of me and blanks out the world around.

"Bad night's sleep?"

I grimace at that. "Hard to tell."

"Why?"

"Sleep's no friend o' mine."

"Do you have bad dreams?"

I shift in my seat. We're getting a bit close to truth now. "I don't dream."

"What? At all?" This seems to shock her, I don't know why. I stopped dreaming when I was very young, and can only vaguely remember what it was like.

"I go to sleep, it goes black. At some point I wake up again." Or I think I do. I'm never really sure. Half the time I'm dressed and outside when I wake. I can never tell if anything's real or just a dream, but they're bloody boring for the main and why can't my brain take me somewhere nice for once? The few dozen streets round where I live, plus churchyards, parks, pubs and alleys aren't exactly inspiring, but that's all I ever get.

"Is this because of the drugs?"

That annoys me for some reason and I snap, "It's cos something's broken in my head, alright?"

"Right. Okay, sorry. I didn't mean to upset you."

I can see from her face I've frightened her, but I can't find the words to apologise. They all seem to jumble up on my tongue and I can't get any of them out—the Three Stooges of apology, wedged together in a doorway.

I get up and start to drift away. When you've scared someone like that, putting some distance between you is the best thing. Right above the words 'paranoid schizophrenic' on my face, she just added one more: 'dangerous.' She could be right too, I'm hardly one to judge.

I shuffle out of the café, ignoring her calling something after me and—

—and I open my eyes. The view isn't pretty. I'm kneeling in a dusk-shrouded churchyard and I wish I was praying. I close my eyes again, hope the devil takes me away from this, but before I do I catch a glimpse of a window out the back of the churchyard. There's a dark outline reflected in it and I hear a chuckle race around the nettles and goose grass choking the graves. It's hard to make out because there's a more pressing sound, the huffing grunt of some overweight Mediterranean man getting off. He's got a grip like a vice and almost tears my ear off as I instinctively jerk away. His other hand's around my throat and pretty soon I'm choking, but mercifully that seems to be what he's into and while it feels like an age, he finishes before I pass out.

"Fuck was that?" he says as he steps back, hands on his hips in a pose of classic male pride. "You were keen enough before."

Fortunately for me, I can't speak and alternate between gasping and retching for long enough to get my wits back. The man's not just fat, he's heavily built too. Kneeling on the ground, I'm an easy target if he doesn't like any of the words running through my head. At last I make myself sick and he makes a disgusted sound and walks off as I crouch on all fours staring down at a puddle of my own misery. It isn't the first time this has happened, I'm sad to say, but at least I know to check my pockets. There's a crumpled note or two in the left-hand one. Not much but I'll say this for the devil, the bastard's determined to get paid before it pisses off and leaves me to deal with the grand finale.

In a little 'fuck you' to me from the devil, my right-hand pocket contains a packet of extra-strong mints and right now I'm too... well, too everything to care about much beyond numbing my tastebuds. My hands are shaking even as I sit on the leaf litter and try to get my head together, but it's full dark by the time I feel I can stand. I head out though the back entrance of the graveyard and cross the road, ignoring the babble of football fans from the pub away to my left. All I can think about is vodka and cigarettes, and the nearest shop provides both.

The man behind the counter has a face that's seen it all before, or thinks he has anyway. Bastard hasn't seen inside my head. I stop as soon as I'm outside and rip open the packet, lighting up as fast as I can and letting the bitter smoke blanket everything as much as possible. That done I glance back and see the man's still watching me. There's nothing to read in his face, neither pity nor condemnation—half his customers are drunks and the other half probably school kids. He'll hate someone like me far less though; however rock-bottom we look we're more likely to pay than those little gobshites.

I'm guessing he's Afghan. I'm no expert, but I know there are a lot of them round here—big surprise after we tear their country apart that no one wants to live there now. Probably he *has* seen most things, but someone like me? I've no idea if I'm even in a club of more than one. Certainly every doctor I ever saw looked pretty surprised when writing or reading the words 'does not respond to chemical treatment' in my file.

Doctors are an egotistical bunch for the main, so when they read it they tend to assume the other guy was just not good at their job. Then they look at the doses I've rocked my way through without my psychosis skipping a beat and most of them stop at being surprised. A few have decided to be rockstars and blitz the problem, but they always fail. Typical, really, the one thing I'm good at is failing to respond to treatment right up to the point I fall into a coma. That happened once, true story, but the devil got its hands on the settlement money.

The Afghan doesn't hold my attention for long, however. The windows of his shop are brightly lit, but above it there's a flat where the windows are dark. Dark enough for a reflection in the streetlights. On the left there's a white hooded figure, on the right a face in shadow. The devil's wearing its usual lazy smile, the angel's face I can never see. The angel doesn't talk to me. As with all God's servants, it's big on watching and judging rather than helping out.

But maybe you get the delusions you deserve, or think you deserve. The angels are that spark of hope, that promise of tomorrow, according to one shrink who did seem to give a shit until despondency took over. White-collar professionals don't much like it when you impugn their skills by failing to get better.

I've never really been able to work out what the angel is there for myself. It doesn't speak, only watches. Occasionally it draws warding symbols in the condensation or rain of whichever window it's reflected in. What good they do I don't know, but they're done when I'm at my lowest, as though some sort of devil's trap will improve my mood. Maybe it does. Maybe just enough to stop me from ending all this shit—the blank periods, the wreckage of a life, the cruel voice in my mind.

Things don't seem so bad with a smoke, I've always thought so. I was a long way from a careless amble back to the doss house, but with a smoke to focus on the rest of the world can go hang, while an awkward shamble feels that bit more louche. I find my key eventually and let myself into the tiny partitioned-off room that is all my housing benefits can stretch to. For a moment I just stand there, looking down at the rumpled sheets of a single bed and the old school desk that serves as every type of table I need.

There's the usual odour of sweat and feet in the air, despite the faintly obscene novelty air-freshener on the windowsill, but all in all this is a safe place

I'm usually glad to see. There are no mirrors, of course, and one indulgence the landlord has permitted is my covering the window with frosted sticky plastic. Normally it's used to stop nosey bastards looking in your front room, but it serves my purposes pretty well and for reasons I can't work out, the devil's never tried to rip it off.

On the desk is a sheet of paper bearing crabbed, awkward handwriting. This stops me dead—it's not a note shoved under the door or an official letter but something left deliberately on the desk. While the devil's rarely written anything down for me, it has the most unfathomably ornate penmanship you could imagine. Its letters take me hours to decipher and I know them as well as the dark reflections that haunt me.

This is different. A child could've done this, but I don't know any children and at the top of the paper is my name.

Adam,

Blessed are the servants of God. Blessed are you who numbers among them, for you were chosen for a burden few could bear. I am the one you call Angel, rendered silent in the presence of the adversary, but charged to be the custodian of your mind. For it is no mere demon of the spirit within you, it is a demon that fights with all its strength to escape the prison of your soul. You are the—

The world goes black around me. Maybe I fall, maybe not—all I know is that my mind's suddenly elsewhere, forcibly dragged into the dark emptiness beyond which is sleep. It's never happened like this before and for the first time in a long while I'm truly terrified. Fear in its many forms has been a constant companion in my life—that hammer of chemicals through the bloodstream that jacks you up as hard as coke and the sudden, shocking realisation of how much your body wants to live.

I know fear, and it'll still turn me into a shaking wreck, but this terror's different—it's one of the soul. It's the realisation that there's nothing beyond this life. It's the sight of yourself as a speck of dust amid the vastness of space. It's the mind untethered and absent from the body that cocoons it. The terror fills me, oily, cold and sluggish. What fragments of my thoughts remain are drowned by it, silently choking until that last spark is gone and there is... nothing.

* * *

When I wake there's pain, a line of fire traced around my ribs, blood dripping from my nose. I lean forward and cough, trying to spit out the iron tang in my mouth only to find myself strapped back, and the effort only intensifies the pain in my ribs.

Slowly my eyes return to focus. A darting blue light, a haze of orange, dancing threads of green—all to the tune of crackling static. Right in front of me is a dark shape, a car seat I finally work out, which means I'm in the back of one, not moving. My head's hurting and my eyes are blurry, but it's about now that I notice that my hands are cuffed painfully behind my back and the blue light is sweeping around the street like a police car's.

Oh shit.

I turn as best I can. The bloody seatbelt's managed to lock in the way they tend to when you want to move and I can't twist very far. Either that or the cops have a way of fixing it in place when they've arrested someone—child locks for criminals.

I can't tell where we are, only that it's late in the night. Some narrow corner of a quiet street—darkened shop-fronts and warehouses all around. I don't recognise it, which means either this is a dream or I must've walked for miles to get here. In the road behind me there's a policeman, a tall, pissed-off-looking guy with a split lip. He's got his baton out and I think I've just worked out why my ribs are hurting so much. There's broken glass on the road, the window of some tatty hardware shop scattered in a million tiny pieces at his feet.

I sit back. The pain in my ribs is too intense to stay like that. It's only then I notice that I can see him in the car's side mirror still. A sickly creeping sensation slithers down my neck. The policeman kicks angrily at the glass at his feet, scattering shards with his heavy boots. Before I can gather my thoughts a dark shape slips onto the mirror's surface, overlaying the reflection there. The devil looks angry now, lips drawn back to reveal the small points of its teeth.

"You don't get to talk to the angel," the devil hisses at me. In the background the policeman's footsteps on broken safety glass sound like the crunch of tiny bones. "You get only me. There is no respite, no succour and no end, do you understand?"

Unexpectedly the devil chuckles. It's a sound I know only too well, one that heralds a new twist or trick it's learned to make my life a living hell.

"There's only one way out of this—surely you realised this by now? There is only me and I am your torment. Witness my punishment."

I feel ice in my guts as the devil disappears. The note from the angel—suddenly it all comes back. What did it say again? I can hardly think straight, my head's hurting too much for me to recall the fleeting glimpse I got before the devil took me. Something about fighting the confines of my soul?

I don't get much time to think. One moment the devil's gone from the mirror, the next it's standing beside the policeman—tall and bulky in a brutal, potent fashion. It's robed in shadows that shift and evade me as I try to look at them; mostly it's the hellish orange sodium glow of its eyes shining through the dark that I see. The devil cocks its head at me and I can see the glee and anticipation radiating out like heat off a furnace. I'm paralysed, struck dumb by shock and fear. I've never seen it standing in the street like that, always just a head and shoulders standing close to the glass it's reflected in.

I've never seen it rip a man's throat out before, either—swift and brutal, the wet sound of tearing flesh and the patter of spilling blood. The policeman collapses, his blood black under the weak streetlights and welling out from under his hands as he clutches his wound. The blood runs fast as I scream and puke at the sight, but I can't turn my head away, can't move other than to shriek, until he's down and still.

"You know what your problem is, Adam?" the devil says into my ear, as soft and intimate as a lover. "Your problem is you're a fucking martyr, right to the bone. And that's nothing to do with me, it's all you. You're the sort of loser who believes deep down that he deserves all the shit that comes his way."

I try to move, but the seat belt has me in its stern embrace and I can barely squirm. The devil's breath is hot and rank on my cheek, the sickly stink of a dead thing that makes me want to gag again. I feel a hand on my shoulder and almost piss myself with fear.

"Now don't get me wrong, you *do* deserve it. God would hate you, but the truth is He doesn't give enough of a damn to feel anything for you. You don't matter enough for that."

I look madly around for some way to escape, but there's nothing. The handcuffs dig into my flesh with a sharpness that's almost welcome—it's real, a tangible pain I can understand. The seatbelt tightens with every movement until I'm pinned right back, arms twisted behind me. In the mirror the corpse gives one final twitch, but my gaze is dragged to a high, dark window of the building opposite. There the angel watches me, silent still—witnessing my descent, its inaction proof of God's contempt.

"But what *would* He hate?" the devil continues, sounding like it's enjoying the captive audience. "Perhaps the fact you've made nothing of your life, sure. Perhaps your absence at church, He's notoriously childish and jealous, after all. But my money's on something a little more basic. Your life's a prison, your existence a joke, but you've not got the guts to do something about it. Year on year I get stronger because you're so weak at heart and all you do is put up with it."

In the distance I hear the sound of sirens, a clamour of noises ripping the quiet of night apart.

"But now you're a cop killer," the devil purrs, "and I'm going to sell your body all 'round whichever shithole prison you end up in."

I hear a click behind me, the scrape of claws on metal, and suddenly my hands are free. There's a clunk in the car door beside me and it slips open. I look around as the sirens get louder.

"Last chance, Adam. Plenty of broken glass round here. You can make it quick if you like, there's always got to be a choice in my game. Door number one has your arse being torn apart year on year, door number two is scattered over the road right now—quick and almost painless."

I struggle out of the car, almost falling as my shaky limbs refuse to obey. Just then a line from the angel's letter appears clear in my head. *'The prison of your soul.'*

Finally things become clear. A long way too late, but I was never a quick study. Real is what you make of it, the kindly shrink said that to me once. Maybe he was wrong about that, dead wrong.

"I'm already in a prison," I croak as I stumble over to the dead cop. A quick search of his pockets brings me two wallets, mine and his, and with one in each of my hands I head off to the nearest side street.

The scream of sirens start to echo round the streets and blue flashing lights reflect off the rooftops. I turn the corner and run.

"And you're in here with me, devil," I say under my breath. "It's your pris-on and I'm the warden. So let's see how I can make your stay more miser-able, eh? Because I'm going fucking nowhere, and you're with me all the way."

ONNEN

Paul Genesse

Kyoto, Heian Era Japan, 968 A.D.

The body of my infant daughter, Ayumi, is buried in the Emperor's tea garden beneath a *hinoki* cypress tree. The men who murdered her did not want to carry a crying baby all the way to the river after she awakened in the darkness of the hot summer night. She must have woken from her blissful dreams because the men's sandals crunched so loudly on the gravel in the palace courtyard. The instant Ayumi realized she was not in my arms she let out a panicked cry sending that sharp pain every mother knows stabbing through my heart.

I tried to look at her, give her comfort, but she could not see me as a rough hand clamped over her mouth and began to suffocate her. I screamed and begged for her life, but the men had gagged and bound me when they took Ayumi and me out of our room in the courtesan's quarters.

She's just a baby. I begged with my eyes for the man to stop smothering her. He ignored my silent plea, and tightened his hand over her face. Her little arms flailed, then slowed, and finally stopped. He held her tiny body up for me to see, as if I were to blame for what he had done. Her head hung limp, her lips blue. My worst fear had come to pass. I wished I could have changed places with her, sacrificed my life so she could live.

The men stopped and her killer dug a shallow hole under a tree. Numb and in disbelief, I watched him bury Ayumi. The man didn't even bother to cover her face with a blanket. He piled dirt over her bare skin, then tamped down her grave with his sandal.

When I think of Ayumi now, I smell freshly turned earth and the woodsy-sage of cypress leaves.

I left my infant daughter's grave when the men picked me up roughly and dragged me away. My hands were bound behind my back as they forced me to walk and we left the palace enclosure through the servant gate. They kept to the darkest and most deserted streets of Kyoto and bore no lanterns. Even if the night watchmen saw us, they would not stop servants bearing the seal of the Imperial Regent, Michinaga Fujiwara.

I could not understand why this was happening. Michinaga loved me more than his wives and concubines, and treasured Ayumi above all his children. I was his favorite courtesan and he had said I would join his family and become his third wife. I was the Lady Ryoko of the Sugawara family, not some common whore to be discarded in the middle of the night.

A dog's sudden bark caught my attention. I caught a glimpse of white fur and remembered Ayumi playing with the tiny brown-faced puppy. Ayumi had laughed and giggled as the dog licked her fingers and toes. Now I would never hear Ayumi laughing again. Tears poured from my eyes, and despite my gag, I mewled and cried.

"Quiet. Or I'll beat you bloody." A man with cheap *sake* on his breath whispered in my ear, but I could not stop. His fist struck my face and crushed my delicate nose. I tasted blood as it gushed down the back of my throat. Stunned and choking, I muffled my sobs, the tears soaking into my disheveled hair.

They carried me the rest of the way, searching for something on the bank of the Kamo River.

"There," Ayumi's murderer said.

They put me on an old latticed door with torn and stained *washi* paper. I smelled fresh ink and noticed *kanji* had been painted on it, but in the darkness I could not read them. The door rested on four sacks of rocks, placed in the corners and affixed with cord. They tied me to the frame by wrapping a long piece of rope around my chest and legs. I could barely see the faces of the six men, but I could smell their rank sweat mingling with the fishy odor of the river.

One man noticed my eyes on him. I shook my head, pleading with him to release me, but he turned away. I fought my gag and tasted coppery blood as I tried to speak. The men ignored me. I was finished cowering in fear. My body tensed with rage. I shook violently, trying to free myself. The men lifted the door, then flipped me upside-down. My stomach lurched.

"You will suffer for this! I will have vengeance!" I screamed unintelligible curses through my gag.

The four sacks of rocks shifted and the stones cracked together on the topside of the door. The bonds cut painfully into my chest as I hung there, digging snake-shaped rope burns across my soft skin. I bucked and twisted as the men waded into the river.

Please, Divine Gods, Honored Sugawara ancestors, save me! I prayed.

The men heaved me toward the deepest part of the channel. The cold water shocked me as I hit the surface. The river took me, rushing water filling my ears. Panicked, I fought against the ropes with all the strength I had left. The skin on my wrists tore and white-hot pain added to my terror.

The rocks pushed me down and I sunk to the bottom of the river. My face smashed into thick black mud where fish guts and sewage collected. Grit stung my eyes. It went into my nose and mouth as the gag prevented me from closing my lips. Water burned as it went down my throat and into my chest. I screamed and the last of the air escaped from my lungs.

Blind and alone in the muddy darkness, I sheared off the fine skin on my wrist and pulled one bloody hand free. Hope surged. My heart pounded in my ears and the searing pain in my chest became unbearable. I clawed and tugged at my bonds, but the door pinned me down. No matter how hard I struggled I could not free my body. My movements slowed as the strength in my limbs failed.

My eyelids closed. The rage I felt for the person who had ordered my death filled my soul with fiery wrath. This was not my end.

I floated in the river, free from my bonds. The blackness of the water filled with a pale blue light. My skin, white as snow, glowed from within. The path to the afterworld of Jigoku opened before me as the yawning maw of a demon. I felt an insistent tug on my soul, but I would not depart the realm of flesh. I surged upward and broke the surface of the river surrounded by a blue glowing mist. Higher still I soared above the slums of Kyoto with the all-consuming need to find who had ordered this dark deed and make him pay.

Fury, sadness, and a desire for vengeance guided what was left of me to the Imperial Palace. The wardings and prayers set upon the walls and gates did not slow the angry spirit I had become. I found myself inside the quarters of the Imperial Regent where I wandered the dark halls. No footsteps on the hardwood floors or *tatami* mats betrayed my presence, but the servants smelled the stink of the river when I passed their rooms and shivered from the cold.

I found Michinaga Fujiwara sleeping in his opulent bedchamber with Meishi Minamoto, his youngest wife, who had always been jealous of me. I loathed her and the red silk and golden trim she had insisted be used to decorate Michinaga's elevated bed.

I could sense his troubled dreams, and his intense guilt. I knew that Michinaga had ordered my death, but why? My instinct was to smother them both as they slept, but that would be too easy. I would make them suffer for the rest of their miserable lives and drive them mad.

I scraped my muddy hands on the walls and watched them flinch in their sleep. I stained the stark white rice paper on the doors with blood from my wrists.

Michinaga pulled a sheet over his shoulder as the sweat on his skin chilled in my presence.

I looked deep inside his dream.

"Do it tonight," Michinaga said, as he relived giving the murderous order.

"Both of them?" the lowborn servant, the one who had killed Ayumi, asked.

"Yes," Michinaga said, trying to hide his regret, and did I sense shame? "Sink them in the river in the manner I ordered. Everything is prepared."

"Yes," the servant said, then hesitated. He opened his mouth to speak, to perhaps ask why this was being done, but Michinaga cut him off.

"Never speak of this again."

"Yes, Imperial Regent."

I could sense Michinaga did not want to face the reason behind his actions. He hid it deep within his mind. I would have to use trickery to learn the truth, so I took control of his dream. His guilt-filled dream of ordering my death vanished, and we were now in his private chambers for our first liaison. I appeared at the peak of my beauty, a young, fresh woman wearing a light turquoise kimono decorated with white flowers. He smelled peony perfume and admired my perfectly coiffed hair piled atop my head.

"Lady Ryoko Sugawara," Michinaga said, addressing me as if we were well acquainted, "I have looked forward to this night."

I bowed low, the porcelain skin on my cheeks turning pink at his compliment, just as he would have remembered it. "I am most honored to have been chosen to be one of your courtesans."

He read me a trite love poem composed for me that afternoon. I smiled and showered him with praise while hoping his skill at lovemaking was better than his tepid verse. He put down the scroll, grabbed my wrists, and pulled me toward him. We kissed tentatively. When he pressed for more I guided the dream to the place he would never forget.

Michinaga recoiled, a look of horror on his face as he tasted river mud from my mouth. He stared at his hands covered with the dark blood from the torn flesh of my wrists.

"What's wrong?" his voice trembled.

"Don't you remember?" I said sweetly, innocently.

He slid away, wiping the blood on his robe as he gagged from the taste in his mouth.

"I am Lady Ryoko Sugawara, your courtesan these past three years. I bore you two daughters. Don't you remember? Our firstborn is perfect Seishi. Where is she now?"

Michinaga shivered. "With my children at my country villa."

"Michinaga-sama, do you remember the promise you made to me about Seishi when she was born?"

"Yes," he said, then noticed the drops of blood at the corners of my mouth where the gag had cut me.

He tightened his lips, realizing this was no simple nightmare. Using the power of my will, I compelled him to speak.

"I promised to arrange for Seishi to marry an emperor," he said.

"Yes, and you will not harm her, like you hurt our second-born, little Ayumi?"

"Not Seishi. Never."

"Why did you have me and our second daughter murdered?" I asked.

He shook his head, eyes full of regret.

"Tell me." I stood over him, blue flames erupting inside the many lanterns in the room, one small echo of my depthless anger.

Michinaga's gaze darted among the lanterns, then he fixed his eyes on mine, perhaps afraid to stare into the ephemeral flames overly long. "Your family has asked me to rule in their favor regarding a land dispute against the Minamoto family. The Sugawara clan needs to understand they are not important and have no influence in the capital."

I read the lie in his aura. Intense shame prevented him from giving me more than a partial truth. I pressed him for more. "You wanted to appease the Minamoto, so you had your youngest daughter suffocated?"

He swallowed, glanced down, apparently unable to meet my gaze any longer. "That's not what I wanted."

"Do you know what they did to me?" The flames touched my eyes. "Your most beloved courtesan and the mother of two of your children?"

He shielded his eyes with bloody hands. I thought he wanted me to kill him and put an end to the disgrace he felt.

"Look at me!" I shouted, my voice a typhoon of hate. A freezing wind burst from my mouth, knocking Michinaga down hard. The wooden floorboards and walls rippled like water in a pool during a storm, tossing him about as if he were nothing.

Michinaga Fujiwara controlled the Emperor, the majority of the noble families, and was the richest and most powerful man in all of Japan, but in the world of nightmares I was a Divine Empress of Fear.

He raised his eyes to mine and I cast off the beautiful shell of who I once was. Lady Ryoko Sugawara was gone. My wet, stringy, black hair hung unkempt and floated around me, dripping river water on his polished floor. Blood ran down from my torn wrists, and my hands became claws the color of mud. I floated in the air above him and threw open my soaking and torn kimono to reveal the rope burns across the bone white flesh of my chest, stomach, and legs.

"*Onryo*, please, do not kill me," Michinaga begged.

I had indeed become an *onryo*, a wrathful spirit of malicious hate. He would tell me why he had me murdered in due time, after he had been punished. "See what you have done?" The words gurgled out of my throat.

I attacked him like a gust of freezing wind. I pushed Michinaga down and locked my mouth over his so he would experience what it was like to suffocate and drown. My tongue split into three eel-like tentacles of icy flesh. I held open his mouth as he screamed into mine. I widened my jaw until I covered his nose and mouth. Eye to eye, I vomited sewage, fish gut-tainted river water and mud down his throat in an inky stream. I filled his lungs until they were near bursting, then forced the filthy water and mud into his stomach, expanding his gut until the skin was tight as a drum. His lungs exploded and his belly ruptured, spilling his water-logged entrails.

The Imperial Regent, Michinaga Fujiwara, woke up from his nightmare vomiting a frothy black liquid. He screamed and flailed as he soiled himself at both ends. Lady Meishi Minamoto shrieked as he attacked her, marring her once perfect face as he nearly gouged out her eyes.

Servants and guards stormed into the bedroom with swords drawn. One slipped on the wet floor, and all trembled at the strange blue light coming from the lanterns. The gibbering Imperial Regent peeled off his filthy robe and crawled into a corner where he trembled like a beaten dog. Lady Meishi fled in terror. It took the full staff of servants the rest of the night to clean the room, though the smell of the river lingered until the end of summer.

Michinaga fled the city that night. I spent my days watching over my surviving daughter, the perfect and beautiful Seishi. She was only two years old, but she knew I was with her. The Fujiwara servants looking after her knew as well. Each one of them who dared raise a voice or lay a hand on Seishi suffered terrible nightmares. I warned them with cold, threatening hands pressed against their throats. I whispered promises of misery and death if they dared harm Seishi.

When I was not haunting and eventually murdering the six men who had drowned me in the river, I passed most of my nights in the Imperial Palace. I wandered the residence of the feeble teenage Emperor Reizei, who had sat on the Chrysanthemum Throne as Michinaga's puppet for less than a year. Since the Regent's departure I made certain the young Emperor could not sleep and found no peace. Every night when he closed his eyes he smelled *hinoki* cypress leaves, and heard the incessant crying of an infant. The sharp, earsplitting wail that drove young mothers insane, and caused infanticide in the lower classes, plagued his Imperial Majesty.

"Search every room!" he shouted to his bewildered servants.

They looked night after night and none of them could find the source.

"Esteemed Emperor," his Major Domo said, forehead pressed against the floor after a long and difficult night, "no infant currently lives in the Imperial Enclosure."

None living. I wanted to make the smug courtier swallow his own tongue for saying such words. He knew. They all knew there had been one infant, but she was gone, disappeared with her inconvenient Sugawara mother. No one would even mention my name. They pretended I had never existed. Only Reizei could hear the cries, while everyone else whispered that their Emperor was going insane.

I came to the desperate young man after he had endured nine straight excruciating nights. He writhed in his bed, tearing at his hair and covering his ears. His face twisted in agony as Ayumi wailed inside his mind.

Reizei moaned and opened his eyes when I brushed my hand on his cheek. I knelt beside him wearing a beautiful purple kimono covered in cherry blossoms, showing myself as a sad young woman of great beauty. He pulled away and stumbled to a window to feel the breeze on his face.

"Honored Imperial Majesty," I whispered, "the gods have sent me to help you."

He fell to his knees. "Please, I beg you. Make it stop."

"You hear the spirit of my daughter, Ayumi. She was murdered in the palace on the orders of Michinaga Fujiwara. She can find no peace."

"Please, there must be a way."

"Her body is buried somewhere here. I wish I knew how to find her," I lied to him, enjoying the game. "Perhaps if she were buried in a proper tomb and the funeral prayers said, she could move on."

Reizei spoke to me late into the night, and on many nights to follow. His servants and all three of his young wives heard him whispering to me. They despaired, as he was alone, talking to shadows.

I reveled as the Emperor searched for Ayumi's grave. Reizei harangued the gardeners to find the body of an infant and had them digging in all the gardens. The courtiers and ministers began to avoid the Emperor and everyone realized Reizei was mad. The priests said openly that he was haunted by a dark spirit. All of the high ministers whispered to each other that Michinaga's choice for Emperor had been a poor one.

When Reizei began to dig in the gravel courtyards and gardens himself, the Imperial Regent was summoned. Michinaga arrived surrounded by Buddhist priests who compelled me to keep my distance. Reizei was forced to abdicate; the broken young man had not even reached his twentieth year. He retired to the country in humiliation to live with his young children and his disgraced wives. I visited him in the last month of summer during the *Oban* festival when the spirits of the dead were welcomed home for their annual visit. I tormented him with the shrill sound of a crying infant, and convinced Reizei he had to puncture both his eardrums with a sharp skewer and deafen himself. His servants found him bleeding from both ears, but sleeping peacefully. I never visited him again, and though deaf, former Emperor Reizei lived a long life in exile.

The new Emperor, the son of a prominent Fujiwara woman, was the eleven-year-old brother of Reizei. The boy was given the name of Enyu, and was enthroned inside the holy *Shishinden* building as hundreds of important officials waited outside in the stifling heat of the palace courtyard. I watched from the rafters and knew this little boy could someday marry my daughter. He would likely have at least four Imperial Consorts, and Seishi could be one of them.

Michinaga kept Emperor Enyu under his firm grasp for many years, but I visited the boy in his dreams. He smelled cherry blossoms and I showed him how beautiful my Seishi was going to become, and promised I would always watch over and protect him from his cruel Regent.

I mostly avoided Michinaga, allowing him to feel safe in the palace again. I needed him to choose Seishi when the time was right. If he was replaced or murdered, there was little chance of my daughter becoming Empress.

When Enyu turned seventeen and the list of consorts was being created, I knew the time was right. Seishi was only twelve, but I wanted her name to appear on the list. I watched a formal meeting between Michinaga and Enyu as they discussed the women who might become an Empress, or the lesser title, Imperial Princess.

"Honored Regent," Enyu said, "I have a humble request."

"Yes, Imperial Highness." Michinaga's brow raised dubiously.

"For as long as I have served as Emperor, I have seen visions of a maiden."

"Who is this maiden?" Michinaga asked.

"At a recent visit to your villa, I saw her."

"Who?"

"Your beautiful daughter, Seishi."

Michinaga flinched and lost his tranquil expression. "Imperial Highness, she is not worthy to be a consort of an Emperor."

"Honored Regent, she is a Lady of the Fujiwara family, your very own treasured daughter."

Michinaga's face soured. He left Enyu without bowing. The rudeness of Michinaga's behavior made me want to tear his flesh, but instead I visited Seishi and waited for her to nap during the heat of the afternoon.

"Honored Mother." Seishi bowed in her dream, her body trembling in my presence.

"Daughter, a good life was denied your sister, but your fate will be different. Never doubt me."

"You honor me, Mother."

I brushed a stray hair away from Seishi's face. My daughter shivered at my touch.

Days later—I do not know how many, as time passes differently for the dead—Enyu answered a summons and met Michinaga inside the hallowed Shrine of the Mirror of Yata within the palace enclosure.

Many priests blessed and cleansed Enyu and his entourage as they entered. The young man was escorted deep inside by an old woman, the daughter of the long deceased Emperor Daigo. She brought him to the inner sanctum and said many prayers in the name of the solar goddess, Amaterasu Omikami, who had given the Mirror of Yata to the Emperors of Japan. She then wafted smoke from an incense cauldron over Enyu before bringing him to a round altar where one of the Three Sacred Treasures of Japan was kept. Lantern light reflected off the polished metal surface of the eight petals of the chrysanthemum-shaped disk. The priestess wore gloves as she lifted the relic and displayed the ancient *kanji* on the back side, which predicted when the Maiden of Heavenly Enlightenment would return.

Michinaga stepped out of the shadows. The priestess remained as the Regent fixed a hard gaze on Enyu. "Do you know what power this treasure bestows?"

"Honored Regent, it bestows wisdom."

"Yes. Wisdom. I hold the power of the Mirror of Yata. It is for me to decide important matters of state. You will marry whomever I choose for you."

"Yes, Honored Regent." Enyu bowed humbly.

Michinaga lifted the mirror and it reflected his face in the shiny surface. I hovered behind him. For a moment I let him see my pale and twisted visage beside his. My eyes filled with hate and my wet hair reached toward him like angry black vipers.

He dropped the mirror and the relic clattered on the table.

"Imperial Regent!" The priestess took the mirror, wrapped it, and put it inside a wooden trunk.

Michinaga bowed curtly before departing.

That night, I waited for everyone to leave the Shrine of Yata. Emperor Daigo's daughter would not depart. She guarded against me, praying and wafting incense. I attacked her spirit, eroding her will and draining her life force. She fought me with prayers and sutras. My spirit weakened. If she could hold on until the sun rose, I would be overcome by the light.

Finally, I whispered to her about Michinaga, and how he did not honor the shrine, or the Mirror of Yata. Her anger at him opened a crack in her resolve. I slipped in like a knife in the back. For the first time in years I inhabited mortal flesh. I felt the pain of an old, arthritic body and smelled aloeswood incense. I hungered for rice.

Despite the weakness in the venerable priestess, I managed to pile ancient scrolls along all four of the outside walls. I lit many candles and started several fires. I left Daigo's daughter when the flames had engulfed the roof. She was a worthy opponent and I could not allow her to live and threaten me in the future. She made no sound when she caught fire. Nor did she run. The old woman knelt down and prayed as the inferno engulfed her and destroyed her shrine. The flames spread quickly as embers were carried on the wind. By morning the entire Imperial Palace was ablaze, and by midday it had burned to the ground. The tree over Ayumi's grave was untouched, as I stood by to douse any ember that touched the trunk or leaves with my wet hair.

Perhaps because of Daigo's daughter's final prayer, the Sacred Mirror of Yata was not destroyed. It was blackened to such an extent that it reflected no light—a grim omen for the Emperor's reign. The court knew of Michinaga's visit to the shrine, and some said he was to blame for the fire. The Goddess had rebuked him and called into question his wisdom as Regent.

The Fujiwara family appeared in force to quash the rumors. Several of those who opposed Michinaga were given posts in the distant north, or found themselves bleeding to death in their bedchambers.

I watched the rebuilding process of the palace begin immediately while the Emperor lived in a lavish villa owned by the Fujiwara clan. He married Koshi Fujiwara, and she was made his first Empress. Seishi's name was not added to the list of his potential consorts. I fumed and skulked, but I did not neglect Enyu. I kept Seishi alive in his dreams. When he lay with his new bride, or any woman, I made certain he thought of Seishi.

First Empress Koshi became pregnant three times, but I filled her insides with stagnant river water and killed the babies. Koshi's servants suspected a curse when they saw and smelled the foul water, but they failed to stop me.

Four years later, Enyu requested Seishi's name be put on the list again, and that she be considered as his next Empress. She was sixteen and her beauty was flowering. They had even written love poems to each other, and once even spoke, through a screen, and with chaperones as was proper.

Michinaga responded by forcing Enyu to marry Nobuko Fujiwara, who officially became his Second Empress. Michinaga proclaimed the girl would soon provide an heir.

My fury erupted when Michinaga moved into his wing of the newly re-built Imperial Palace. I entered his bedchamber through the floor. I flung a lantern against a rice paper wall and the fire spread hungrily. Michinaga woke up gasping and coughing. My dark eyes fixed on him and he saw me clinging to the ceiling, my wet hair steaming as the flames engulfed the room.

As he fled, I chased him down the hall, my claws cutting through his robe and leaving long red scratches across his back. I pinned him down and held him as the fire consumed the ceiling. Cinders fell on his legs and Michinaga shouted. "I'll tell you! Please, spare me!"

Would he reveal why he had murdered me at last? I released my hold.

Michinaga scrambled to his feet.

"Tell me," I said.

His expression showed humiliation at what I'd done to him. He opened his mouth to speak, but shook his head and fled as the palace burned. Was it his shame or, more likely, malice toward me that kept him silent?

Once again the courtiers, their army of servants, and all their guards had to find other living quarters, this time during a particularly cold winter when peasants froze in their houses for lack of firewood.

The people of Kyoto read dark portents in this event. Michinaga tried to keep it from them, but the people learned that half of the mirror of Yata was melted, a stark portent proclaiming the waning wisdom and power of the empire.

Over the next two years the palace was rebuilt again, at the expense of the long-suffering people, the Fujiwara clan, and others eager to earn the favor of the most powerful family in Japan. Enyu was compelled to accept two more wives: Junshi, the daughter of Emperor Reizei, and Onshi, a Fujiwara daughter. Both were given the title of Imperial Princess.

My daughter, Seishi shared my sadness. I visited her at night as she wept quietly. As I approached, the tears on her cheeks froze into tiny ice crystals.

"Honored Mother." She bowed.

"I am sorry, daughter. Emperor Enyu will not take another wife. You will never be his empress."

"I could be his concubine."

"You will not. You were to have the honor and the protection of being an empress. I have failed you, cherished Seishi, but I will make Michinaga pay when he returns."

I was the only occupant of the Imperial Residence during the reconstruction, as no servants or builders would dare stay there at night. Even the guards on watch remained outside. They had seen me many times roaming the halls and gardens. Sometimes I even sat on the Chrysanthemum Throne. I called to the spirits of the dead servants and courtiers who had perished in the two fires. They assembled to pay homage to me and I formed a court of the dead.

My time as the unchallenged ruler of the Kyoto Imperial Palace ended when six thousand Buddhist priests dressed in white robes entered the gates from all four directions. Like an army they marched in lines, two by two, chanting sutras, dispersing incense, and ringing bells. They blessed and cleansed the grounds. The spirits of the dead servants were quickly sent to Jigoku to face judgment.

I, however, resisted easily and fled to Ayumi's grave beside the *hinoki* cypress. Her spirit had long since passed, but her bones empowered me. I waited as many priests filled the garden. They sat in the lotus position and prayed. Many glanced toward me as I hid by the tree. Did they know I was there? Or did they know the location of my baby daughter's grave?

The deepest level of Jigoku was reserved for those who killed holy men, but I would murder them all if they tried to take Ayumi's remains. I stood guard late into the night as they maintained their own vigil, repeating their prayers.

"Lady Ryoko Sugawara."

After midnight, I heard my name and felt a tug I could not ignore. Someone had summoned me to a newly built structure I could not remember ever having visited. A bare-chested priest with a bald head sat in the center of a large square room with a high ceiling where bright white lanterns hung. Dozens of monks sat in an open gallery overlooking him on the second and third floors, chanting and praying in unison. Hundreds more priests outside the building joined them in the courtyard, but I could not understand their deep-throated words.

The line between the world of the living and the dead blurred as I entered the hall. The rich scent of *byaku-dan* incense made from sandalwood trees surprised me, as I had been unable to smell anything since I possessed Emperor Daigo's daughter. I suddenly realized I was rooted to the ground. I felt the smooth wooden floor with my feet, and heard the swish of my soaking wet and cold kimono. Had I been drawn into the mind of this priest? Was I inside his waking dream?

My dread increased when I noticed a section of the floor had been removed in front of the priest, revealing the circular shaft of an ancient well.

The blackness of the pit called to me and I walked toward it with small, tentative steps.

I knelt at the edge of the shaft and looked into the depths. Waiting for me at the bottom was the gate to the deepest layer of Jigoku where I would be tormented endlessly. I would be pierced with a thousand white-hot needles, scalped and flayed, torn apart by ravenous beasts, and crushed flat in a cycle that would last until I was reborn. All of which could take hundreds of years, perhaps more.

In shock, I realized I had been brought into a trap. I looked up at the motionless priest on the other side of the well to measure my enemy. He sat cross-legged, hands pressed together under his chin as he prayed silently. His entire body was covered with the characters for the heart sutra. The words ran down his body in dark lines of ink. As I read bits of the prayer on his skin I understood the low chanting around me at last.

"Form is not different from emptiness. Emptiness is not different from form. Form is indeed emptiness. Emptiness is indeed form."

The monks chanted the prayer, stanza after stanza, the words creating a barrier between myself and the priest. I could not touch him, and I felt my resolve fading. This was not a battle I could win. In this place, the power of six thousand Buddhist monks' collective prayers compelled me to go into the well shaft and depart forever.

If I could not defeat the man in front of me, their holy champion, their exorcist, I was lost.

"In the void there are no forms and no feelings, conceptions, impulses and no consciousness."

I stared at him with an unblinking hatred, though he would not open his eyes and face me. The *kanji* for wisdom was painted prominently on his forehead. I wanted to reach out and strangle him, but the heart sutra repelled me.

The longer I sat, the harder it became to defy the coercive force urging me to step into the well. I finally manifested enough strength to crawl around the lip of the pit and reach the other side. I sniffed at the priest like a wolf, searching for a weakness. Even the soles of his feet were marked with holy *kanji*. I reached for him, trying to break the warding, but my hands could not make contact. Even the water from my hair dripping toward him was repelled like rain striking an invisible rooftop.

I tested his defenses during hours of uncounted recitations of the heart sutra. If I could not defeat him before dawn, the light of the sunrise would be my end. I would be cast into Jigoku.

"There is no truth of suffering, of the cause of suffering, of the cessation of suffering or of the path. There is no wisdom, and there is no attainment whatsoever. Because there is nothing to be attained."

The chant rumbled on like an endless line of tsunami waves battering me down. I had to fight.

"I'm not afraid to kill holy men," I whispered.

Then I noticed the unmarked flesh of his ears. No *kanji* had been painted there.

I stood triumphant behind the priest. I focused my strength and penetrated his aura, grabbing onto his ears with iron-cold hands. My fingers dug into his flesh, sharp fingernails piercing his skin. I screamed like a howling wind—the last sound he would ever hear—and tore off both his ears.

He did not flinch as blood gushed from the puckered holes in his skull. Many of the monks stopped chanting, and I kicked the earless exorcist into the shaft. When he hit the bottom and broke his neck I slipped out of his dream.

The lanterns above me exploded into bright orange flames. The ceiling caught fire. Frightened monks tried to flee the balconies. I sealed the doors with my hate and fanned the flames. The white robes of the monks charred and turned black as each of them lit like candlewicks.

"Burn!" I screamed and showed myself as I flew toward the ceiling.

Dozens of priests died in agony as the third great fire in six years swept over the palace. I watched the army of priests flee, but I was not satisfied with driving them away. Cold wind carried embers aloft and started Kyoto ablaze. I watched the fire spread from district to district.

The smoke cleared three days later. The city was a charred ruin. I found a young monk weeping beside the river. His body was weakened from hunger and sorrow. I possessed him and I walked to the destroyed shrine where the Mirror of Yata had been kept. I found the lump of blackened metal buried in ashes.

"You will carry this to Michinaga Fujiwara," I told the young monk. "Tell him the Lady Ryoko Sugawara says these words: 'The wisdom of the Emperor is gone.'"

The fire destroyed the winter food supplies and the people of Kyoto suffered great famine. When the snow covered the city a starving man tried to harvest fish from the koi pond near Ayumi's grave. I clawed the skin on his face and chest, and sent him running for his life. No one entered the ruins of the palace after that. The city rebuilt slowly. The gardens grew wild in soil enriched by ashes. Tall weeds choked the courtyards. My enemies cowered, not daring to look at the scorched walls of my domain or pass the wrecked gates.

The second summer after the great fire I received a visitor. The humble priest waited at the servants' gate for three days and nights, fasting and praying. I came to him at midnight. He could see into the spirit world. He prostrated himself, showing great respect. "Honored Lady. I am Juten of the Zojo-ji Temple. Please may I speak with you?"

"If you can find me," I said, then disappeared.

Juten walked into the maze of fallen buildings overgrown with weeds. He found his way to the cypress tree and knelt down, head bowed.

"You may speak," I said, impressed.

"Honored Lady. I have come on behalf of your esteemed daughter, the Lady Seishi."

The mention of her name made the sadness inside me much sharper.

"She wishes for me to bring news."

"Speak."

"Honored Lady, she has been filled with despair these past years. The man she loved, Emperor Enyu, has been forced to abdicate the throne by the Imperial Regent. Enyu has taken the tonsure and become a monk. Michinaga Fujiwara has chosen a new Emperor, former Emperor Reizei's eldest son, Kazan."

"Will Kazan have the palace rebuilt?" I asked. "Will he come here for a crowning ceremony?"

"Honored Lady," Juten said, "Emperor Kazan will do nothing here until the matter of your unsettled spirit is resolved."

"They know what I want. Michinaga will have Emperor Kazan marry my daughter and make her First Empress."

"Forgive me, Honorable Lady. It is believed that a marriage will not settle the situation. A marriage alone will not give to you the respect and honor you deserve. Nor will it calm the *onnen* within you."

Onnen. The potent mix of fury, sadness, and the desire for revenge had brought me back from the dead and sustained me for years. "*Onnen* cannot be calmed. It is eternal."

"Honored Lady, your esteemed daughter and the people of Kyoto recognize that you must be revered as a goddess. Lady Ryoko Sugawara must be worshipped for all time as a goddess of fire and wrath. A great shrine must be built for you on the grounds of the Imperial Enclosure. We believe that you will protect us in the times ahead from flame and ruin."

"What about Michinaga? What does he believe?"

"The Imperial Regent understands the importance of this matter. He has agreed wholeheartedly and will personally provide all of the funds required. You will be deified, and a lavish shrine constructed."

"He wants my daughter to marry Emperor Kazan?" I sensed a trap.

"Honored Lady, yes. Kazan was chosen to follow Enyu long ago."

"Where is Emperor Kazan?"

"The Emperor is in the Golden Villa outside town."

"Remain here," I commanded, then left to find the new Emperor. It was easy enough to start a fire outside the opulent home. The young Emperor was overcome by smoke and his servants carried him outside. As he lay unconscious on the grass I entered his mind. He was a full year away from being twenty and had a vicious temperament toward women, handling them roughly. I knew immediately that Kazan would brutalize my daughter.

Emperor Reizei had other sons, and I found them all that night. His second son, Sanjo, was the half-brother to Emperor Kazan. Young Sanjo was a kind boy of sixteen who composed beautiful poetry. He did not take life or privilege for granted. His eyesight was failing, and might be entirely gone before long.

I returned to the priest, Juten of the Zojo-ji temple. "I have made my decision."

"Yes, Honored Lady."

"Inform Imperial Regent Michinaga that Emperor Kazan will abdicate the throne and take the tonsure. He has been judged as weak. As a cloistered monk he will not have women to abuse. Have Michinaga make certain Kazan does not find other distractions of the flesh in the monastery."

"Yes, Honored Lady."

"My daughter will marry Kazan's half-brother, Sanjo. They will wed here in the palace, which will be rebuilt to look exactly as it did before with one exception. There will be a large shrine built and dedicated to me around the tallest *hinoki* cypress tree in the main garden. My daughter will be the head priestess, and her eldest daughter after her."

"Yes, Honored Lady." Juten bowed, and asked permission to carry the message to Lady Seishi. He departed as dawn broke over the eastern hills.

I thought for the briefest of moments that I felt the heat from the sunrise.

Emperor Kazan abdicated under duress and spent the rest of his days in a monastery under a vow of silence. His half-brother Sanjo was seated on the newly crafted Chrysanthemum Throne a month later. Days after Sanjo's ascension, he married my daughter, Lady Seishi Sugawara, making her his First Empress.

I watched the Imperial couple enter my newly built shrine. They made ritual offerings of rice and water, and said silent prayers. I found little of the sadness had gone from my soul, and I would not release my grudge against Michinaga Fujiwara. He refused to enter my shrine and pay proper respect, and I heard him say he was "unworthy." He retired to the country, renouncing his title as Regent and leaving the court forever.

I visited him that first night and asked, "Will you tell me now?"

"I cannot. I made a vow."

"We shall see." I twisted his dream into a grim nightmare. A dozen cold and wet hands reached up from under the floor and pinned him down. Mud flowed from ceiling and slowly filled his bedchamber.

"Stop! Please!" he shouted as he was buried alive.

Michinaga woke up vomiting river mud.

The next night I possessed the sleeping body of his newest concubine, a dim girl from Osaka. I wrapped my arms around his neck from behind and began to choke him. Michinaga woke up and lashed out. He rolled and fought desperately, finally grabbing a vase and bashing in the girl's head.

After she died, his concubines and wives were terrified of being near him at night. I watched as Michinaga became isolated and paranoid. He would often awaken with his clothing wet and stinking of polluted river water and his own incontinent bowels.

I tormented him for almost twenty more long years. Michinaga's mind was nearly broken at the venerable age of sixty-two, and I put water from mosquito-infested pools inside his lungs. The insects hatched inside him and tried to escape. He writhed and whimpered as the bugs crawled out his nose and mouth.

"Ryoko, please kill me. Then I will tell you," he whispered as I clung to the ceiling above his bed one night, letting murky water drip from my hair onto his skin.

I fell upon him and filled his stomach with thick mud that hardened into clay. I watched him starve and drown as he suffered great pain over the next few nights. When he was about to die, I floated over Michinaga's bed and held him down. I forced my long wet hair down his throat and into his lungs. He died gasping and choking as he stared into my angry black eyes.

I seized his soul and took him to the capped well shaft inside the palace that led to Jigoku.

"Please, Ryoko-sama" he said, "I will tell you now."

"It does not matter," I said. "Only your suffering matters."

"I shall suffer in Jigoku for what I achieved in this life."

"Tell the truth, then!" I shouted.

"I did not want to do it, but to keep my position I had to show my family and my enemies the strength of my resolve."

"Your resolve?" My eyes burned with hate.

"The Fujiwara clan asked me to sacrifice the one I loved most, and if I did, I would be Imperial Regent for as long as I chose."

"Sacrifice the one you loved the most?" I did not want to believe him, and had almost forgotten he had once proclaimed his love for me and our youngest daughter. For all those years I thought his words had been a cruel lie.

"My family read my poems. They knew it was Ayumi and you, Ryoko-san. I consented to your sacrifice to satisfy them. They believed in the old ways, and had to be appeased. The most dishonorable act of my life secured my position of absolute authority. I was too ashamed to speak of it before in case you would forgive me. I deserved a lifetime of suffering. I wanted you to punish me all these years. I welcomed it, and I endured the punishment because I loved you, and little Ayumi." He fell to his knees, his eyes filled with tears. "Ryoko-san, I am so sorry. Please, forgive me now."

Despite the truth of his pitiful words, the chill in my heart did not thaw. "Do not think this is over, Michinaga. I will see you again." I threw him into the well, disgusted that he claimed to have loved me. I no longer had the ability to forgive or love him.

The fury I felt did not fade, even after my daughter birthed six children, one of whom became Emperor Go-Ichijo. The offerings of water from mountain springs cooled my anger at times, but in the thousand years after my death, there were periods when I was not properly venerated.

I burned the royal palace and Kyoto eight times to remind the people the price of forgetfulness. My shrine always survived the destruction and to this day it sits in the Imperial Enclosure surrounded by a beautiful garden and *hinoki* cypress trees. The secret shrine is tended personally by the descendants of Empress Seishi.

The Imperial family finally fled the haunted Kyoto Palace over one hundred and fifty years ago, and no one resides there to this day, though the grounds are kept just as they were when I walked as a living woman. Oblivious visitors stroll the grounds during the day and are told lies about the supposed unbroken line of beneficent Emperors.

Historians and poets all fear to speak of me or write about my life. Lady Ryoko Sugawara, the Goddess of Fire and Wrath, the mother of Empress Seishi, has been forgotten by most of the world, but at night the Imperial Enclosure is mine alone. No one dares enter as they fear the cruel power of *onnen.*

I still wait for Michinaga to be reincarnated, and when he returns, I will haunt him for another lifetime, and then another. There will never be an end to his suffering.

TO DREAM AWAKE, TO SLEEP THE REAL

Michaelbrent Collings

So many people think that dreams die when you wake up.

The reality is this: the dreams *begin* with waking eyes. It's just that those dreams aren't necessarily the good ones.

This was what Booker Nyx knew well, and what he had thought many times in the years since he had married. His wedding stood out in sharp lines and stark, bright colors. A series of moments so real and so clear that they could be nothing but reality, nothing but truth. The flowers, the dancing, the wine, the song. The cake that tasted so sweet and felt so sticky when Lyssa smeared it all over his face and then shoved some up his nose for good measure. The drive home, slow because he was a bit buzzed but still moving as fast as he dared because he wanted to be alone with his bride, the woman who had, for some unknown and unknowable reason, agreed to be Mrs. Nyx.

They made love. They whispered.

A beautiful time. Eyes half-shut in that place reserved solely for those most in love—or perhaps for those most insane, which might be one and the same. Dreamless, every moment experienced to the last atom of its reality. And that is, indeed, the definition of insanity: to understand the world so perfectly that the rest of the universe looks askance. They think you strange, they whisper about you in the dark. They fear you, and what you have.

Booker Nyx started to think he might be insane, early on in his marriage. Perhaps not merely in love, but mad.

Two people, passing through life, eyes half-shut. Existing with one foot in dream, and the other in a place where the world was seen as it truly was: a place of magic, and wonder, and light, and infinite possibility.

Yes, madness, to be sure.

Then the children came. The eyes drifted fully open. The madness disappeared and the dreams began.

Eyes always open when children arrive. There are simply too many things to guard against for a good parent to allow half-closed eyes. That, Booker realized, was why so many parents fall out of love when the children come. They stepped out of the reality of magic and infinite possibility and into the dreamland that came with sleep deprivation and midnight feedings and so many smelly diapers that you took the stench with you everywhere you went. They moved from a place where they heard what *was* (silence, broken by the real sounds of lovers whispering as raindrops pattered rhythms on the roof) to what *might* be (ghost cries of a baby who wasn't really awake, but whom you feared *would* be awakened by the thunderous crashing of raindrops on the roof).

The children opened Booker's eyes. They made him tired. He was awake, but dreaming. The dreams killed the beautiful reality.

Lyssa turned from lover to mother. No longer *his*, but *theirs*. And though she insisted he was one of the people that still mattered, he knew it wasn't true. His eyes were open, he was dreaming, and in this dream as in so many others he was always running toward what he wanted but never really making progress.

So... he ran after money, and never quite reached it. There would be *just* enough in the bank, and then the dream would wrinkle a bit and a car would break down or the roof would leak or one of the kids would need braces.

So... he ran after better jobs, and never quite reached them. He was promoted occasionally, but always after the dream bent to provide first for someone younger, someone less qualified. Someone who was the right color or the right sex or the right orientation or the right shoe size or the right this that this that this that blah blah blah.

Most of all, he could no longer reach Lyssa. She lay beside him in the bed, but far away. Nursing a child who came between them, then another and a third. And then the children were grown too large to nurse but they still came in, still interrupted nightly. "Mommy, I have a problem." "Daddy, my tummy hurts." "Can you get me some water?" "Can you help me find my pink blanky?"

Booker thought about killing himself. But he had heard that if you died in a dream you died in real life, and if that was true, would he ever find his way back to that sleepy place he had once loved? Would he ever find reality again? The sweet, mad verity of bliss and lovers' kisses?

He lived. He watched. He dreamed.

"Daddy, I have a splinter."

"Mommy, I think my hamster died."

"Why can't *we* stay up late?"

Then the children were teenagers. And now there was nothing between him and Lyssa. The days were long, and exhausting, and Booker was glad. Glad because maybe now the nights would bring back half-closed eyes and sweet whispers. Nothing in the world but him and his beautiful wife and the Real.

Yeah. This is it. This is where we fall asleep and things go back to—

"Why are you looking at me like that?"

Booker blinked. Lyssa was frowning. That little side-of-the-mouth frown she had when she was deciding how mad to be. He took too long to respond —easy to do in the wake/dream state of life—and the frown moved from side to full-center. She had decided to be all-the-way irritated.

"I said, why are you looking at me like that?"

Booker fell back on the usual safety tactic of married men: "Just thinking how pretty you look."

Lyssa responded as married women everywhere had responded since time immemorial: Derisive laugh.

He sighed. Got into bed. By the time he was under the covers Lyssa was back to what she had been doing: watching a show on her tablet. Tiny, tinny sounds escaped from the earbuds she wore, the ghosts of actors' voices. It reminded Booker of those many nights, those many years, of jerking awake to every sound on the baby monitors. Wondering if he would have to get up or if he could go back to sleep. But of course he never went back to sleep.

Sleep was for the non-dreaming.

"*Merrily, merrily, merrily, merrily, life is but a dream…*" he murmured.

"You say something?" said Lyssa. Her voice was only half-present. Just as much a ghost as the voices of the medical drama she watched were to Booker. Some nurse banging some doctor while some patient died of some sad combination of brain cancer and irritable bowel syndrome. He didn't like those shows.

"Just singing a song to myself."

"That's weird."

"Sure is." He looked at her tablet. Said cancer/poop patient was expiring in a way that would bring an Emmy to the attending physician—or at least to his perfectly-upswept hair. "You really like this stuff?"

She sighed. Removed the earbud closest to him. "I can barely hear you." It was her way of saying, *Do you want to talk?*

"Go back to your show. I'll be quiet."

She did. He was.

A moment later Gabby poked her head in the room. "When do *I* get a tablet?"

Booker put a finger over his lips and then lay his head on his flattened hands: *Shut up and go to sleep, little girl!*

But Gabby wasn't that little. Sixteen and just as dream-addled as everything else around here. She thought she deserved everything, and—worse—thought everything was possible. Which made her either a genius or a fool. Judging by her report card, Booker didn't have much hope for the former.

"You and mom both have tablets. You get to watch whatever you want, whenever you want. Why not me?"

He answered her as he always did: "Because you're not old enough. It's not a good idea for kids to have those things."

She argued. He listened. Lyssa breathed out exceptionally hard every once in a while to let them know their argument was intruding on her study of Tourette Syndrome/erectile dysfunction patients.

Gabby stalked off. The other kids came in, and both Kevin and Madison somehow found a way to work their need for a tablet into their goodnight wishes. Nicer than Gabby, but still insistent, with the veiled threat of increased teenageriness if their demands were not met.

When did being a father turn into a crash course in hostage negotiation?

Eventually Booker turned off the light. The room didn't darken completely, because Lyssa was still watching her show. Or maybe it was another one. Some police procedural where a mad serial killer who hated the world because his mother had been molested by a rodeo clown and was now out to murder all hookers who smelled like sweaty bulls.

The light from Lyssa's tablet danced through the otherwise dark room. Made it seem like not merely a place of Dream, but of Nightmare. Even when he closed his eyes, the lights pulsed through in dim pinks and purples and the occasional brighter flash of red. The show was still there, the fantasy in a dream.

He slept.

Only the sleep wasn't real, of course. His eyes still had to be open. Gabby had started trying to sneak out of the house, and Booker remained awake. The dream-state of exhaustion and life as it had become followed him into the night and chased away whatever chance he might have had of returning to the fantastic sleep-world of the Real.

"I found a *deeeeeeeal!*"

Gabby was on the family computer. The tower and monitor sat in a corner of the kitchen, right in the middle of every possible lane of traffic. That had been something Booker insisted on. He didn't want the computer cloistered off in a private place, somewhere that the kids could be on it, doing Heaven-only-knew-what without any threat of accountability. The trade-off was that now he couldn't hide from hearing about everything they did: Minecraft creations, new Facebook updates, the most recent celebrity scandal involving someone's selfie.

"What is it?" He leaned over her shoulder and groaned internally. She was on some website that purported to sell electronics at prices so low they were impossible. Which they were, of course. "Honey, this is just a scam."

"No, it isn't. You can bid on stuff and win quality merchandise for ridiculously low low prices."

No, my dear, the ridiculous thing is that you are actually quoting from their sales pitch to convince me.

Out loud Booker said, "It doesn't work that way. You bid, sure, but they have computers always bidding you up. So at the last second you find out that what you're really paying if you want the stuff is pretty much the full price."

He saw what Gabby wanted, of course: a "Family Tablet Package"—five of the latest tablet computers with one year of high-speed roaming. Permanent connectivity. "YOU COULD HAVE THIS AS LOW AS 1$!" it screamed in letters that blinked and changed colors.

"Look, the dollar sign isn't even on the right side of the '1,'" he said.

"You're focused on *that*?" Gabby said. "The deal of the century and you're focused on a typo?" She rolled her eyes and with the simple gesture managed to convey the complex thought that she believed him to be the dumbest hominid ever to somehow drop out of the trees and exchange poo-flinging for a nine-to-five job.

He felt anger—the rage that was more and more his constant companion in this waking dream—rising up. "Fine," he said. He shoved his daughter out of the way. She started to raise hell about that until he said, "Do *you* have the credit card to register?"

"Oh, Daddy!" she screamed, and threw her arms around him.

The registration took only a few moments. He had his credit card number memorized—a sad testament to how much he had to use it. Then he entered his item number, and the last information to be provided: "PLEASE FILL IN MAXIMUM BID?"

This time Booker didn't point out the error, even though turning a sentence into a question grated on the English professor in him. He just filled in his maximum.

"A *DOLLAR*?" Gabby screamed. "You have to fill in more than that!"

He crossed his arms and shook his head. "Why? If it's the deal of the century this should be plenty. I expect to get some change, actually."

"Dad, don't be such a—"

"Gabby, shut up." Her mouth clapped shut so fast he heard her teeth clack together. Those were not words typically heard in this house, a house where "talking out differences" was the rule. But he was tired. So tired. And he just didn't want to deal with her nonsense. "This will be a good lesson for you. You'll see how high the bidding goes, and how much tablets cost, and maybe then you'll *get the HELL OFF MY BACK.*"

The roar sounded louder than it probably was in the otherwise-silent kitchen. Lyssa and the other kids were at Kevin's baseball game, so there was no one to reprimand him for his loss of control. Gabby seemed to sense she might be out of her league. She shrank away.

The computer beeped. The bidding started.

It was a fast bid. Only ten minutes. Booker's bid went up first: **SandmanB —$1!**

Nine minutes later it was the only bid. "We're gonna get it!" said Gabby.

He sighed. "No, we're not. I told you: they have computers that wait until the last minute, then they auto-bid you up. Either they get you to bid full price or they outbid you and keep the merchandise for another sucker."

Nine minutes and thirty seconds.

And forty seconds.

And fifty.

The computer beeped. Words appeared.

You Have Won The Family Tablet Package!!!

Booker couldn't believe it.

They don't need three exclamation points. Just one is enough. More than that is redundant. What moron wrote the copy for this website?

His thoughts were an avoidance. He didn't want to look at Gabby. He didn't have to. He could feel her smirk, hot on his neck, then his cheek. She moved him aside—much more gently than he had done with her. Entered their shipping information. Then she clicked the logout button. "Wouldn't want anyone to get your information or anything," she said. "People get scammed that way."

She moved away.

"Merrily, merrily, merrily, merrily..."

Booker sat, alone in the kitchen, singing the same four words over and over until Lyssa and the other kids came home. Lyssa asked if he'd gotten dinner ready. He hadn't. She was annoyed.

"... life is but a dream..."

* * *

Two days later Booker was working on the couch, grading papers written by a bunch of students whose parents had enough money to get them into a good university, but not enough sense to insist their kids learn basic English. Always frustrating, and looking at the graded pages—most of which had more red on them than a slaughterhouse floor at closing time—made him wish he'd just killed himself after his honeymoon. Less paperwork involved in suicides.

Someone knocked, the sharp triple-rap of someone who cares only for the knock itself and not so much about whether it is answered or not. Booker was only ten feet away from the door, but by the time he got there he only saw the last flash of a brown van disappearing around the corner of his street.

A plain white package sat on his porch. A red strip with the words "Second Day Delivery" emblazoned across it wrapped around the outside. There was no return address.

Booker took the package inside.

Gabby was standing in the living room. She should have been at school, but there she was, grinning and grabbing for the box.

"It's *awesome.*"

"So fast!"

"Look at this! The display! You can see their *pores!*"

"Ewww! Who wants to see close-ups of sweat?"

Lyssa sat on the couch, Gabby and Madison on either side of her. Kevin sat at their feet. All four of them held tablets, all four of them stared at different images on the little computers.

Madison was playing a game based on some animated movie that Booker still hadn't seen. Dragons and pixies and a big monster that looked like a banana with a steroid addiction.

Kevin was engrossed in a live-stream of a baseball game. Chicago was ahead.

Gabby was tapping the screen, fingers moving so fast he could barely see them. Social media. "Social" meaning that she was silently interacting via the perfect filter of ones and zeros with someone who lived six houses away. Tablets and typing rather than phones and faces.

Lyssa... the doctor with the upswept hair was busy saving someone whose heart had exploded through his big toes.

Booker sat on a nearby chair and looked at the fifth tablet. It was nice, no doubt about it. Sleek and black and cradling easily in his hands. The glass screen untouched by human fingers, unsmeared by use. A thing so new he was hesitant to spoil its perfection.

It stared at him. A dark void. A window.

An eye.

He put it aside. He still had papers to grade.

Everyone was quiet the next morning. No screaming at breakfast about who had finished the milk, who got to pour the cereal first. No anxious hustle out the door with shouted acrimony accompanying the trip to the high school.

Gabby actually said *words* to him when he dropped them all off. Granted, they were "Geez, Dad!" but that was still better than the sullen silence he usually got.

Booker's classes went well. Most of the students in his classes were clearly more interested in their next sexual conquest than in their next literary triumph, but some of them managed to write coherent sentences. A victory for Western culture.

He came home. The house was quiet. There was peace. It was late enough that everyone should have been back from school/work/sports/mall/skipping school, but he figured Lyssa must have taken the kids out for pizza. Generally he hated when she did that—money was tight enough without unscheduled trips to restaurants they couldn't afford—but tonight he was glad. He enjoyed the silence, the quiet that he thought just *might* lull him back into that silent sleep of the Real.

He went into the kitchen, thinking he might grab himself a quick snack. Not hungry for dinner, but an apple or some chips might be nice. He'd blow off papers for tonight and read a book.

How long since you did that? Just read for the pleasure of reading?

Too long.

The kitchen was dark, but he made his way across a space as familiar to him as his own body. Opened the fridge. Grabbed a Granny Smith and turned... and a small shout leaped out of him.

Gabby was sitting at the kitchen table. He hadn't even noticed her there, sitting in the darkness, absolutely still. The only reason he saw her was the pale yellow of the refrigerator light, casting dim fronds across the kitchen, turning his daughter into a jaundiced ghoul.

The tablet was propped up in front of her. Dark. Silent. The glass reflecting nothing, not even his daughter's face. For a moment he was gripped by the feeling that Gabby wasn't really there. That what he was seeing was just a ghost; a wraith. A thing long dead but still remembered.

"Gabby?" She didn't move. Just kept staring at the nothingspace in the depths of the screen. He said it again, louder. "Gabby?"

This time she heard. Her body shook, a shiver that writhed from legs to head. She turned her head toward him, her face blank a moment too long. Then her eyes focused. "Dad, hi!" she said. She smiled at him, and the sense of unreality deepened. He couldn't remember how long it had been since she smiled like that.

"You okay?"

"Yeah, fine. I was just watching..." Her words petered out as she turned back to the tablet. "Huh. I musta fallen asleep." She turned back to him and grinned once more. "All work and no play, huh?"

"Yeah. You eat?" It was all he could think to say. The moment was so strange that his mind had defaulted to a Parental Essential: "You eat?" "Bedtime!" or "Don't give me that look!" were almost always safe comments.

Gabby shook her head. "No. Not hungry, really." She looked back at the blank tablet. "I kinda want to finish my show."

A chill swept through Booker, a shard of ice that made its way through his guts, searing them with its cold. "No!" The shout came too loud in the dark kitchen. The night itself seemed suddenly unsettled. "No," he said again, quieter. "Just let me put my stuff down. I'll make us something."

"Sure!" she said. Another smile. "I'll be right here."

He nodded and went to his room.

What was that *about?*

He threw his coat and satchel on the bed. Didn't even turn on the light, just tossed them into the darkness so he could hurry back to his daughter.

"Oof! What—?"

He had already spun back to the hall, now he continued the turn, making it a complete circle so he ended up facing into his room once more. He flicked the light switch. The bulb flared to life, illumination chased the shadows from the room.

Lyssa was sitting up on the bed. The satchel had landed on her legs, the coat had flapped its way across the room to land on her chest. They dropped off her as she sat up, the satchel falling open and papers spilling out.

"Why'd you throw those on me?" she said.

"Sorry, I didn't—I didn't know… Were you asleep?"

She looked around. Shrugged. "I must have been." She blinked and wiped her eyes. That was when Booker realized she was holding her new tablet in her other hand.

"Were you watching something?" he said.

She noticed the tablet as well. Shrugged. "I really can't remember." She put the device on her bedside table and spotted the clock. "Is that the time? I have to get dinner going!" She stood and rushed out of the room. She shouted for the kids as she went, and by the time Booker got to the kitchen Kevin and Madison had come out of their rooms as well.

Everyone was in the kitchen.

Lyssa was cutting onions. Booker had no idea what she was going to make.

Everyone was there. Together.

Merrily, merrily, merrily, merrily….

It was only later that Booker realized that, though every member of his family was in the room, they were not together after all. Sitting beside one another. Smiling. Happy. But not speaking, not even looking at each other.

No, not together. Alone.

The smiles were silent and far away, as though each was enjoying a favored memory. A joke they had heard.

Something they had seen on a glass screen.

Lyssa watched one of her programs that night. Earbuds came with the tablets, and Booker heard her show not at all. The ghosts were silent. There was peace.

He stared at his tablet a long time. The power button was on the side.

He didn't push it.

He put it away.

He rolled over and closed his eyes without turning off the lights.

Lyssa laughed at something on the small screen.

Then she was silent.

"Dad, why don't you use your tablet?"

Booker looked up from his papers. It was nine o'clock and the work he had avoided last night somehow *hadn't* magically disappeared or been done by benevolent pixies. So he was back on the couch in the front room, hunched over endless-seeming pages of borderline competence.

Madison stood in front of him. She was holding her tablet in both hands, moving her fingers as she played her dragon/pixie/overmuscled banana game. Her eyes roved over the screen so quickly it looked like she was in an open-eyed REM state, upright dreaming.

"I don't know," said Booker. Which was a lie. He didn't use it because it unnerved him. Made him feel like the dream of his life was shifting, becoming something darker than it had been. The blurred lines between love and hate, between anxiousness and excitement, were sharpening.

But the dream of his life wasn't going back to the sleepy reality he remembered. It was becoming something else. Something he didn't like. Didn't want.

"You should check it out. It's really a good tablet."

"Okay."

Madison nodded. Mission accomplished. She never looked at him. She played for another moment, then turned away and walked out of the room. Booker looked back at his papers at the same time, so he almost missed it.

He jumped off the couch. For the second time in twenty-four hours the papers scattered. He ran after his youngest daughter. "Madison!" he shouted.

She was already in the hall. The door to her bedroom shut as he was entering the corridor. He strode toward it. Opened it.

Madison was in bed. Covers up to her neck. Eyes shut. Asleep.

Life is just a dream....

The tablet was nowhere to be seen.

"Madison?" he said.

She didn't answer.

Booker stood there for a moment longer, wondering if he had really seen what he thought he saw.

Madison. Fingers moving over the touchscreen. Smile on her face as she played.

And nothing on the screen.

Booker went to Kevin's room. Just down the hall from Maddie's. He opened without knocking.

Kevin was in the dark room. Not in his bed, but at his desk. Staring at a dark piece of plastic and metal and glass.

He swung to look at Booker. Smiled a wide smile that Booker had worried for years would be the downfall of many girls. "What's up, Daddy?" he said.

Booker left. Running. Moving so fast it barely registered that Kevin had called him "Daddy."

When did he call me that last? When he was ten? Eight? Younger?

The other side of the house. Gabby's room.

This one was bright. The lights on. But that just highlighted how dark was the screen she stared at.

She smiled as well. A smile more beautiful than the one she usually graced him with. "Yeah, Daddy?"

This time he noticed the appellation immediately. That cold shard jabbed at him again. His stomach curled, he had to consciously keep from doubling over.

"Yes, Daddy?"

"Nothing."

She smiled even more brightly, then turned back to her empty tablet.

Or maybe not empty. Maybe it's just playing something I can't see. Something I don't want to see.

Booker finally went to his own room. The door was locked, and for a moment he wondered if Lyssa was in there with another man. The only reason they'd *ever* locked their door was when they wanted a mid-day quickie and needed to make sure none of the kids barreled in on them.

And how long's it been since that happened?

So maybe she was in there enjoying a moment with someone else.

The idea was strangely comforting. Because that would make sense. It would be explainable. It would be a return to the waking dream of his life.

He pulled the key from its resting place atop the doorframe and turned it in the lock. Twisted the knob. Threw open the door.

Lyssa was in there. On the bed. Nude.

She is *having an affair.*

The strangely incongruous hope died as fast as it was born, murdered by the sight of the rectangle on her bare stomach. No affair after all. Not one of flesh and bone, at least. Not one that made sense to Booker.

Lyssa's eyes were open, but she was not watching the tablet. Her hands traced lazy circles across the glass, then drifted over her own skin. Breathing quickened.

"Oh, Book," she said. "Why don't you watch? Why don't you join us?"

He felt like throwing up. Not just because of what he was seeing, but because of the sudden urge to do what she wanted.

He didn't understand what had come into their home with the electronic devices. Didn't understand the change they brought. But it was horrifying, and terrible, and so... so... attractive.

Her breathing grew faster and faster. She writhed on the bed. He couldn't tell if it was pleasure or pain that made her twist like that.

Other breaths sounded behind him. The children.

They stepped past him. Each bearing their rectangles, each wearing their smiles. Booker couldn't stop staring. The sight of his wife, turning naked on their bed while their children walked toward her with Cheshire grins, transfixed him.

The kids lay hands on her. Breast, forehead, leg. Lyssa quieted.

The tablets turned on.

Booker looked. He saw.

He fell into the lights.

He fell, suddenly and completely, asleep.

So many people think that dreams die when you wake up.

The reality is this: the dreams *begin* with waking eyes. It's just that those dreams aren't necessarily the good ones. But now Booker was asleep, now he found what his family had found. He found the Real. The illusions of life peeled away, to reveal the nothing beneath the nothing.

This was the Real: the dream below the dream.

Twisting in the Real, Booker still had no idea what had brought the tablets. But he knew now that it had brought his family an understanding of the nothing they had become. And that was freedom. Why try to be a family? They could dissolve into the separate worlds they wanted, could divest themselves of the illusion of unity. And, in so doing, perhaps Lyssa and Maddie and Kevin and Gabby had found their happiness.

He woke for a moment. Saw that Lyssa was beside him on the bed. The children with him in the room. They were all dead, all bleeding from slit throats and crushed skulls, but their eyes were open and they were present and paying attention to him and him alone.

This was enough. They didn't have to be alive, they just had to be his.

He sank back into the Real, into the nothing below the dream. Surrounded by his loved ones, finally together in a way that only the separation of technology could bring.

He sang.

"Merrily, merrily, merrily, merrily..."

There was a knife in his hands, still sticky.

He looked at the point.

Time to sleep. Life was but a dream, after all.

WHAT HELLHOUNDS DREAM

Steven Diamond

I don't have dreams. I survive them.

It's been nearly forty years since I made a deal with a crossroads demon and became her hellhound. You have to understand that I was in way over my head at the time, barely treading water. Dying. I still remember that day like a reflection in a still pond. You know, when the surface is like glass in the early morning. You have to understand this part, otherwise none of the rest will make sense.

I'd been shot twice, once in the leg, and the other in the stomach. Gut shot. I was leaking blood like a faucet, and those that had done the shooting were on my obvious trail. All of this for witnessing a drug deal. Looking back on it, I suppose it's hard to blame them. Had I survived, I would have brought the whole mess down on them just by being able to identify them.

'Course, I survived.

They didn't.

I couldn't tell you how I made it as far as I did. When I finally collapsed, my body running on the fumes of what little blood was still in me, I was on my back in the middle of a road. A crossroads, it turns out.

There wasn't anything I could do except lie there and wait for my pursuers to find me and kill me. I think at that point I'd just about given up. Next thing I know, standing above me is the most beautiful woman I've ever seen. Her hair was as white as snow, and cut real short. That normally wasn't the type of thing I went for, but on her... well, let's just say I felt every last drop of my remaining blood flowing hot through my veins.

Her eyes seemed all black, and at first I thought it was just that I was near-dead and it being dark and all. Nope. They were all black, no whites. Once I fully took in that tiny detail, that hot blood went ice-cold.

"Looks like you're in a smidge of a mess, hon," she said. Lord, but her voice sounded amazing. "You and I need to have ourselves a discussion, I think. You fancy you can stay conscious for a few minutes?"

"People... after me... catch up... soon." At least that's how I think I sounded. It could have been a slight more rough.

"Don't worry about them, hon," she patted me on the cheek. Gently. Her skin was smooth and cool. "Where we are at, nothing can get to us if I don't want it to. No, don't ask. You keep your breath. Right now it's better suited inside you than out. Turns out, Mr. Jericho Falls, that you landed in my crossroads, and the blood you're spilling summoned me. Lucky you. Probably."

"My name...?" I managed.

She smiled at me, and all I wanted to do was lean up and kiss her. Her canines looked just a bit longer and sharper than they should. "Your blood tells quite a story, Jericho. It tells me all I need to know about you. Name. Family. Past. Present. It even tells me a bit of your futures. That was plural on purpose.

"Let me give it to you straight, Jericho," she continued, settling down on her behind right there next to me in the road. Her road, I suppose. "You're gonna die. Either from the blood loss and that gut shot, or from those men you saw dealing the devil's goods. Let me ask you a question: You wanna die?"

It took some effort, but I shook my head.

"Well," she said with another of her smiles. Were her teeth more pointed? Memory is a funny thing, and every time I think on it, those teeth did indeed seem more pointy than before. "It turns out that I can help you, sweetie. I can give you a measure of power to overcome this. You'll live. In fact, you'll live like you've never lived before. You'll be stronger than ever. Have you heard of a hellhound? It ain't a dog. It's what you'll become.

"You want to know the catch?" she asked me. I nodded. "Good, because something like this ain't cheap. And no amount of money you have now or ever will have will be enough. You came here at just the right time, Jericho, because normally this sort of thing would cost you your soul. Still wouldn't be a bad deal for either of us, but it turns out us crossroads demons find ourselves in need of a man to collect on debts.

"I need you to understand, you'll be ours. My sisters and I have lots that needs doin'. And you'll be the trigger man for it all." She hesitated for a moment then spoke again. "And, hon, not everyone we send you after will be strictly human. You'll do it for the rest of your life. No breaks. No holidays. You do our bidding and become our hound. Or, you die right now."

Let's be honest, what choice did I have? I was just alive enough to respond, and just dead enough to believe every word she said. And when it comes to death, I was and still am a coward.

I nodded once.

"Now that is just splendid," she said. She leaned in and kissed me full on the mouth. I could taste my own blood in that kiss, but it didn't stop her. Seemed to make her a little crazy, even. She pressed herself against me harder and harder until it was nearing painful.

"Ma'am, you may want to back away from that man," a deep voice said. "We'd rather not kill you too."

She pushed herself up from me, blood smeared across her lips like lipstick painted on by an epileptic. "Boys," she said, and her voice no longer sounded nice and sweet. It was full of scorn, blackness, and death. "You have grossly misunderstood the situation."

I didn't see anything. My brain was kinda foggy, and I was fading. But I heard the most terrible sounds. Rending of flesh and breaking of bone. A few times blood splattered me. There were all sorts of screams. The worst, though, was the woman's—the demon's—laughing.

I passed out.

When I drifted back into wakefulness, the crossroads demon was again at my side. This time, though, I was in a bed. She patted me on the shoulder and smiled again. She looked completely normal other than the all-black eyes. The bedroom was well lit, and I could see how pale she was.

"Welcome back, Jericho Falls. How we feeling this morning, darlin'?"

I expected pain, but none came. I was just tired. I said as much, not able to keep the surprise out of my voice.

She laughed and stroked my cheek with a soft hand. "That's because all you injuries are healed. I even took care of those old high-school sports injuries for you. Don't worry, sugar, that part is on the house. You'll rest for a few days, and then I'll send you out. Go live in your home like usual. But don't bother going back to work. Accounting doesn't suit you anymore. Death does.

"There's one thing I forgot to mention last night," she continued. "I hope you'll forgive the omission, but things got a bit... hectic. There's a side-effect to the 'new you' that you're going to discover. When you are about our business—my sisters and me—those experiences and memories never leave you. This is very important, my dear Jericho, so I need you to listen like your life depends on it. Because it does. You listening?"

"Yes, ma'am," I said. Respectfulness seemed appropriate considering I was both alive, and in the presence of a demon that had assuredly massacred those people who had been chasing me.

"Good. These jobs we will have you do, they will stay with you until the day you die. It's the cost of being a hellhound. If you ever dream that you are reliving one of these experiences—and you surely will—they'll be dangerous memories. In your dreams, Jericho, memories are real. You will relive whatever you do on our behalf, and if you fail in your dream, hon, that has consequences in the waking world. Call it a side-effect of being—oh, how do I phrase this for you?—a supernatural fella dealing with supernatural contracts. That make sense? Because of who you are now, and who and what you'll be dealing with, the jumblin' of all that power gets stored up in you. You'll live it forever. Kinda like your own personal hellish nightmare. But real."

I must have had a mite bit of a dubious expression on my face, because she slapped me then, hard as can be. I tasted fresh blood in my mouth, and one of my teeth felt loose.

"This is not a ghost story, Jericho," she said, and those black eyes burned with terrible heat and anger. "This is not a joke. Get a scratch in your dreams, you'll see it in the morning... if you wake. Because if you die in those memories—in those dreams, my boy—you die in life."

I just nodded. I thought I understood. Really, how could I understand any of it until I'd been there and done it?

I sat at home for months, doing pretty much nothing. I was only twenty at the time, and I'd been told to quit my job as an accountant. But I was never short on cash. Like clockwork, every Friday I received a deposit into my bank account for two thousand dollars. Mind you, this was nearing on forty years ago. Two thousand was more than I knew what to do with. 'Course, being an accountant I knew not to blow it all. I invested.

I'm worth a shade north of 10.5 million these days.

In the meantime, I felt best not to remain idle. I worked out every day, and I found I had virtually limitless energy. In those early days, I once ran on a treadmill for five hours straight. I ran sixty-five miles in that span. I stopped because the treadmill shut down on me.

Things didn't stop there. I could see in the dark. My vertical leap was nearly three times my height. I benched seven hundred pounds. I was barely six feet tall, and hardly a buck-fifty soaking wet.

I received my first job four months after those brief moments laying there bleeding out into the crossroads. The job came personally, from the cross-roads demon that had "saved" me. She'd finally told me her name: Savannah. A pretty enough name. It suited her well. She usually talked like she had in those first moments, but I could tell it was an assumed accent. It slipped at times. She delivered the job with a smile and told me that it was a "warm-up." She also delivered a small 9mm handgun with a suppressor screwed onto the barrel.

Now, I knew what to do with a gun, even in those days. I'd always been fascinated by them, and I went to the range a couple times a month. But I didn't own a gun. I certainly didn't own a suppressor.

The job was to be simple enough. There was a young woman whose time was up. She'd sold her soul, was all I was told, and she'd been given ten years from that moment to live life to the fullest.

Here is what I can't wrap my mind around, and still to this day it bothers me: I simply nodded and asked where to go.

That's it.

I should have been horrified. I should have been disgusted with myself that I'd been asked to kill a woman, and that I wasn't protesting. I simply didn't care much. I'm not sure how I got that way. Was it all those months waiting around, just waiting to be called on? Had the boredom conditioned me to be willing to kill a person just to have *something to do?* Or had something inside me been changed when I'd been healed? Maybe something, some of my inhibitions or my morality, had been removed from me along with those bullets.

The woman—her name was Elizabeth Storey—lived in a sprawling, gated home in a town called El Dorado Hills. I flew into Sacramento and drove out to that area in a rental. A quick drive-by showed me the gated walls surrounding the place were only ten feet high. I could jump them, no problem.

I saw a gate house with at least two men inside.

Ms. Storey was paranoid, then. I reckon she had good reason. I was coming to gun her down, after all.

I went in at night, and the instant I leapt over the fence, I felt something inside me. Something hot, dark, and wrong. But it felt kinda right. I was new to the whole breaking-and-entering thing in those days, and I was spotted immediately. Two guards had their guns pointed at me almost as soon as my feet hit the ground on their side of the fence.

Giving them a warning would have been the right thing to do. Give them a fair shot. But the thing running around in me—the other that hadn't been there before my deal with the demon—shut that idea down. Hard. Instead, I surged towards the guards. It's hard to know if they were pros or not. They died too quickly to tell. I imagine that I must have looked a slight bit like a blur as I hit them. One moment I was fifteen feet away, the next I was between them, and then behind them. I grabbed one by the sides of the head and spun him around, snapping his neck. The other I hit in the throat with a jab that collapsed everything there.

It took two seconds. Neither made a sound.

I killed four more guards on my way to Ms. Storey's room in the center of the rambling home, the most protected spot. It made sense. If I were in her position, I'd have done it the same.

When I entered her room, Elizabeth was waiting for me with a gun pointed at my chest. She wasn't angry. More resigned than anything. Tired. She couldn't have been much older than myself. Which meant she was around ten or twelve when she made her deal at a crossroads. A bit of me lamented that fact even as I pulled out the suppressed 9mm.

I stood there, gun pointed without firing. I'm not sure why I hesitated. She had me dead to rights, but she didn't fire either.

"Are you going to shoot?" she asked.

"Are you?" I asked in return.

"I can feel them on you," she said, squinting her eyes. "The demons. Today is my day, of course. It's hard to forget the day you are told you will die."

"How old are you?"

"Twenty-one," she answered.

"So you were eleven when you made the deal?" There was a whole 'nother question there, and she heard it.

"My parents were getting divorced. As a kid, that was pretty much the end of my world. I found a book that told me how I could make a deal with a demon. Seemed like a good idea at the time. Since then I've lived life knowing I'd only have ten years."

It seemed a bit much, truth be told. Is an eleven-year-old really able to make a decision like that? The situation smacked of a little girl being taken advantage of. But what could I do? The crossroads demon, Savannah, was clear that if I ever went against her wishes, I'd be ripped into literal pieces.

I remembered thinking maybe it was best that I let Elizabeth live, and die myself. But then if I didn't do it, who would? A bullet to her brain, quick and painless, from me... or one of the demons comes and adds her personal, bloodsoaked touch.

My way suddenly seemed more merciful.

"You should probably pull that trigger," she said. "My mind is beginning to think that maybe if I kill you I get a few more days to live. That sounds tremendously appealing the more I dwell on it."

I nodded. Her words weren't sincere, just an excuse to get the whole business over and done with.

She set her gun on the table and leaned back in her chair. It was an odd thought, but I couldn't help but notice how comfortable the chair she sat in seemed to be.

Elizabeth Storey smiled at me, then said, "I'll see you in Hell." There was no malice in it. Just a statement of fact. I nodded and smiled too. I felt sad, but this was something that had to be done.

I pulled the trigger.

A month later I had my first dream. I'd done two more jobs in that month, both simple affairs like the Elizabeth Storey thing. But this was my first dream. Of course it had to be a dream about that first kill.

I suppose I didn't really believe Savannah when she told me that my dream memories of my work had real, waking consequences. About that whole business of all that supernatural energy being stored up in me.

So I wasn't worried when the dream started. Sure, it felt absolutely real. Every detail was just as I remembered it, down to the night breeze and the stars that were shining down. The two guards looked equally real. They both had guns drawn, just like the first time.

Only this time, I didn't react fast enough. Sure, I went forward, but not as quickly as the first time. I was careless. One of their guns went off, and the impact took me in the shoulder, very nearly spinning me around. It hurt just like the first time I'd been shot. The shock of the pain made me scream, and I fell to the ground.

Fear descended on me right quick. Savannah's warning seemed drastically understated.

I kicked out, snapping the knee of a guard sideways and in. I drew my gun and snapped a quick shot into the other guard's face, dropping him instantly. I rolled over and put the barrel of my pistol to the first guard's temple and fired.

I laid there breathing heavy for a few moments. I could hear the shouts of the other guards. Is this what things would have been like if I hadn't dispatched these two guards so quickly?

I pushed myself to my feet and walked towards the side door I'd used the first time. I came across the same guards I'd killed before, only they were more wary due to the shots I'd fired, and my scream of pain. Unlike the movies, a suppressor doesn't "silence" a gun. There's still a sound, and if you know what to listen for, it will draw your attention just like a regular gunshot.

I took another graze along my thigh before finishing off all the guards.

When I went into Elizabeth Storey's room, everything went just like it had the first time. We had the same conversation, except her expression was a little different seeing me come in with wounds and blood dripping onto her carpet.

For the second time in a month, I shot her once in the head.

When I woke up, my shoulder hurt like nobody's business. Blood soaked my sheets, and I felt weak.

"Maybe next time you'll listen to me, dearie," a voice said from the corner of my darkened room. Savannah stepped out of the shadows. There was no accusation in her voice, just a statement of fact. "The good news is you'll heal quickly. A perk of being my hound. You'll keep the scars, but you should be ready to work in a week or two. Rest up, hon."

She left then, without offering any more help or advice.

I went into the bathroom and pulled out a first-aid kit. I wiped the blood off and found it leaking from a too-real bullet wound. There was even a bullet, oddly enough. I had to dig it out myself. I keep the slug in my pocket as a reminder.

That was when I learned that I don't have dreams. I survive them.

That was all forty years ago. I'm pushing sixty now, though I don't look or move like I'm a day over forty-five. During that time, though, it felt like I lived the lives of ten men.

I sat at my table, drinking a glass of ice-water with a ribeye I'd grilled—medium—and waited for my next job. I was feeling weary right at that moment. My twenties were spent knocking off people whose time had come. Some were good. Some weren't so much. The ones that bothered me the most were those people that had made deals as kids or for their kids. But what was I to do?

Some folks die with dignity. They don't hold with begging at the end. They lift their chins up. I've had some swear to me that they know they did the wrong thing for the right reasons, and that this is just something else for them to fight. Those are the men and women that make my job worth doing. I realize that sounds odd. But it's the whiners—those that cry, not out of fear, but out of selfishness—that make me want to eat a bullet. Or the ones that made crossroads deals for proud or worldly reasons. The worst are the ones that did it out of malice.

But those individuals that made a bad deal because of the love in their hearts, well, it's right hard to judge them.

A black smudge on my glass made me look at my right hand. There in the creases and scars I found the blood from the monster I'd killed before dinner. I squinted a bit. Sighed. My eyes were starting to go. Soon I'd have to wear *glasses*. A fella in my position really can't afford to have his eyes fail. I'd missed some of the blood, and the sight of it right at that moment made me lose interest in the last few bites of steak.

This last job had been rough. Thing was a minotaur of some sort. Easy to find, hard to kill. Very hard to kill. Though it was certainly harder for me now than it would have been a decade ago.

The monster had tried making deals of its own in the San Antonio area. Crossroads demons don't take too kindly to other things infringing on what they consider their god-given right. Yeah. You heard that right enough.

I wasn't looking forward to dreaming about that bull-man.

See, the crux of the whole dream situation wasn't made truly clear to me until years after that first kill. It wasn't just that I dreamed up those memories and had to survive them again. Nope.

The memories always stayed the same. But I got older in them.

There was a good chance that I'd go to bed tonight and get pulled into a memory from twenty years ago. The memory would be from then. But I'd be as I am now. So not only do I get to survive the dreams, but I have to try and keep up with my younger self.

It is mighty tiring.

I hadn't had a dream for a few weeks, so the way I figured, I was about due. I'm not scared of anything, really, not anymore. But things do give me... pause. The dream-memories are one of those things. There was a time in the early days when I tried not sleeping. I don't need rest like most of flesh and blood, but after two weeks without a wink, I became mighty tired. Sooner or later the sandman wrestles you down, even if you're a hellhound. And of course I had a dream that very night.

Nearly didn't make it out of that one.

My exhaustion from the waking world carried over into the dream-memory. I have a scar two inches thick that runs the length of my spine to prove how close it was. Savannah had to come tend to me personally for a week while I healed up from that dream-memory.

I spared a glance at the digital display on my microwave. 10pm. Savannah never came with new jobs after 10, so I was good to go. And by that, I meant to bed. I needed my rest. Not because of jobs in the waking world, but because of reliving those jobs in my dreams.

And I had a right severe sense of unease. A bad dream was coming.

A nightmare.

I opened my eyes, and immediately wished I could wake up or be in any other dream.

I always know right away when I'm in one of the dream-memories. There's no sense of distortion, and no dream-haze. Nothing overly vivid or under-detailed.

This memory was bad enough when I lived it in the waking world. It was worse the first time I dreamed it. It was pure agony by the twentieth time. This was the memory of my first encounter with supernatural creatures. I had been twenty-five the first time around, back when I was still a tad reckless, and way stronger than I am now. This dream got worse as I got older, because it got harder. Knowing where everything is isn't a guarantee of success. It's like being in the middle of a mile-long tunnel with the train fifty feet away coming at you full-speed. You know it's there, but that doesn't do you a ton of good.

I would have stalled to take a few breaths, but even doing that would put me off my game. My best bet here was to get an earlier jump than usual. Kill everything before they knew I was there. It mostly worked last time.

Over the past forty years, I've gained a healthy disrespect for fae creatures. They aren't like you see them in kid cartoons. They aren't like what you read about in most fiction these days. I believe in God and the Devil—it ain't taken on faith for me. I also believe in the *other* that is disavowed by both of those opposing forces. Some things are just so wild and dangerous that both sides would rather put them down than see them breathe.

I was standing outside an old warehouse in downtown Sacramento. It should have been abandoned. To the normal person's eyes, it was. But to me, due to my added abilities as being a crossroads demon's hitman, I could see the warehouse was in full use. Lights on, smoke billowing out of the top through a vent. I could smell burning flesh. A lot of it. I reached down and felt a kukri strapped to my thigh, just like it always was.

I wished that it was a Springfield XD 5" Tactical. But then, those hadn't been invented yet.

A nice and trusty 1911 would have done nicely.

In thirty seconds a patrol would find me if I wasn't all-out sprinting for an emergency ladder on the south side of the building. In my younger days I'd stalled too long and come into contact with them. They almost killed me then, when I was younger and stronger. I was bone weary these days. I didn't like my chances in a fight with them now.

I ran, and I could feel the breath coming quite a bit harder than when I'd last had this dream ten years ago. What would happen if I died? Would Savannah just shrug and find a replacement? No reason to think she wouldn't. I planted my foot on the wall and leapt fifteen feet to grab the lowest rung on the emergency ladder. I barely got it.

How was I going to survive this?

I climbed to the top of the ladder where it met a metal landing and a rusted door. I pushed open the door and stepped into the warehouse, where I immediately was greeted by a blast of hot air and the overwhelming stench of rotting corpses and burning meat.

I also ran right into the first guard. I'd been too slow.

I'm not sure what these things are even called. Savannah didn't have a word for them in English. In her own language—some corrupted form of Enochian—she said their name loosely translated into "Bodies of Teeth." Yeah.

At first glance it was human enough. If you passed it on the street, you wouldn't even notice except for a maybe a slight bit of a chill. 'Course, I reckon not seeing them for what they are is a blessing. I wish I couldn't see them.

Their legs and arms, when viewed though my eyes, were too long and had one joint too many. But that wasn't the bad part.

The bad part was when it seemed to *unfold* from the forehead down to the crotch.

Dozens of appendages, all looking like wet, dripping spider legs, unfurled themselves to a full three feet. Droplets of blood fell from each with a faint pattering sound onto the metal catwalk we both stood on inside that warehouse. How all those leg parts fit inside the human-shaped meat sack, I still don't know. But the space left vacant by the appendages was a seething mass of flesh and meat.

It jumped onto the wall to my left and attacked. That sort of thing would shock and confuse even the toughest of men. It's why the Bodies of Teeth did it.

I pulled the kukri from where it was strapped to my thigh. I hadn't realized I'd been so slow in getting this far, or I would have had it out already. The only thing that saved me from those stabbing spider leg-things was that I'd been through this variation before. Just once. I pivoted to my left and brought the kukri around in an arc. The blade severed the waving appendages on the thing's right side. A shock of blood sprayed out, coating me.

Dropping low, I cut at the back of its legs as it fell past me silently.

The Bodies of Teeth don't make sounds. It's horrible in its own way, and even demoralizing when you don't have an audio cue to whether it's in pain or not. They just keep coming until they've been hacked or shot to bits.

I was grateful this time for the lack of sound. It meant they didn't hear me yet.

So I hacked away.

In my youthful days I'd been more... artistic with my fighting. I danced around creatures and men, killing them without scarcely being touched. These days I went at killing with a more blue-collar attitude, like chopping wood. And I didn't stop until it had ceased even twitching.

This wasn't even the hard part yet.

I know I'm not a good guy. I do wetwork for demons. Not a lot of redemption in that line of employment. But I try to put some weight on the good side of the scales whenever I can. The opportunities don't come very often, so when they do, I have to make good on them. The part of this job that becomes my own little slice of Hell is when I am reminded of how I didn't do something good when I had the chance.

A flight of stairs led me down to the main floor, and another into the basement. Along the way, the cocoons began appearing. People were in all of them. Men. Women.

Kids.

It would have been one thing for them to be eaten. I can almost deal with that kind of behavior. Monsters eat people. That story gets told all the time in my line of work. I've become used to it, after a fashion. But this? No. This disgusted me on a deep level.

They were being hollowed out, then changed.

The process was outlined, cocoon by cocoon. Step by step. They were hollowed out, bit by bit, but kept alive through the process. I learned later that the part about being kept alive was essential to the change process. How were they kept alive? By being fed, the innards of other people through an umbilical cord of some sort.

It still is the most horrific thing I have ever seen. In my dreams I stopped looking, as if that would prevent my having those images stitched across my retinas.

I was able to surprise two of the Bodies of Teeth from behind, killing them before they knew I was even there. I may be getting older and slower, but I'm still good at what I do. And I have a lot of job experience.

My job was to kill the queen of these Bodies of Teeth. "Queen" is my word. Nothing regal to it, whatever it really is. All I know is that this queen is the one that starts the process. The people that survive are turned into more of the monsters. Those that don't survive are incinerated or fed to the ones being incubated.

When I came to the part of the warehouse basement where the queen was, things fell apart, just like they had originally. The queen was prepping a whole group of people. They'd been split into men, women and kids. The men were all but done, and were being dragged away. A dozen Bodies of Teeth saw me enter that portion of the warehouse. I'd tried a dozen different approaches in my dreams, and none worked. Most were worse, actually. This way, boldly walking in, at least confused them for a second.

I cut three apart before they realized what was going on. Then the rest attacked. There wasn't a whole lot of counter-attacking on my part, mostly just getting out of the way of all the stabbing appendages. The queen had triple the leg-things writhing about. They flared out, likely directing the other Bodies of Teeth.

I was bleeding from a dozen puncture wounds by the time I'd killed the majority of them. I felt one drop on my back, and its appendages stuck into me like a centipede. It hurt like nothing else. As this happened, I got to see my failure.

The queen killed all the women in front of me.

There was a particular gleam in the queen's alien eyes. This was a punishment for intruding. The queen moved from one bound woman to the next, and with a quick stab, ended each of their lives while I was held down.

I reached back, and ripped one of the appendages gripping me from the monster it was attached to. The Body of Teeth pulled itself free of me, flailing around like a grasshopper with one of its legs pulled off. I took the appendage and rammed it into the pulsing mass in its middle. It collapsed like a rag doll.

It took me far longer to kill the rest of the minions than it originally had. I was getting too old for this, and it was just getting worse. Originally, I'd dispatched all the Bodies of Teeth much more quickly, and I'd even saved a few of the children. Not all, but a few. In all my dreams since, I'd repeated that small miracle. It was the only thing that made dealing with this mess over and over again any sort of palatable.

Like I said, I was too slow this time.

I killed the last Body of Teeth and turned to end the queen, turned in time to see her kill the last child.

When I woke up, bleeding all over the sheets, I stumbled to the bathroom and threw up until I had nothing left. Then I dry-heaved some more. And more.

And more.

I was laying there shaking on the tiled floor of my bathroom when I had a horrible thought.

If I could get injured, and even die, in those dreams... what happened when events to other people changed in my dreams?

I've said before that I like to balance the scales every now and again. It keeps a guy like me sane. I knew the names of the children I saved that day. Most had been too mentally and emotionally scarred to do much with their lives. Consequently I'd snuck into many of their funerals after they committed suicide.

I looked up one of the last three living children.

I found nothing.

And I found nothing on the other two.

Then I found an old news article online stating that their bodies had been recovered with the bodies of dead women and men in a warehouse in Sacramento. I was numb at this point. Was that was how it worked? Any good I did could be undone, just like that? With the snap of a finger? What if I never had the dream again, and never got a chance to re-save them?

The impact of the thoughts staggered me.

My heart hammered in my chest, and pain gripped me. I clutched at my left arm and chest, and my vision went black at the edges, until it overtook me.

I woke up, and it was dark outside. Savannah sat at my bedside, looking worried for once.

"What did you do?"

I shook my head, a gesture of both frustration at her question and incomprehension.

"Things changed, Jericho," she said. Her normal accent was gone. A bad sign. "What did you do?"

I told her as best I could, and by the time I finished, she actually looked afraid. "That shouldn't be possible," she said. "How could you let this happen?"

That last bit came out as a scream that tore at the insides of my mind. I felt fresh blood leaking from my ears and nose. I coughed, and felt some blood come up there too. I turned my head and spit it onto the floor of my room.

I didn't have a chance to answer her. She began shouting again, blaming me for unwriting the past. Blaming me for altering her contracts. I didn't catch a lot of it. I was lucky to be conscious. All her yelling took a physical toll on me, though. There is power in everything demon does, and I felt every shout as they literally tore through me.

When she finally left, it only took a few moments for me to lapse back into unconsciousness.

* * *

When it rains, it pours.

I woke up in another memory. Two nights in a row. This had never happened before.

I was complete wreck, but I still had the benefit of being a hellhound. Already most of the minor stuff was healing. The internal damage Savannah had done with her yelling was pretty much gone but for scars no one would ever see.

Here I was again. The memory of my first job.

I should have been grateful. This was the easiest of any job I was ever assigned. But somehow I felt angry. Angrier than I had been in a long, long time. After barely surviving one of the worst memories in my resume, and having seen how my failures can grow even worse, I was now here to experience my first job again. A job in which I still had a whole lot of trouble seeing the justice.

Elizabeth Storey. Maybe it was just all the anger, frustration and guilt I was feeling, but I was convinced now, more than ever, that she hadn't deserved to die. She'd been essentially coerced into dealing her soul away at an age when she couldn't have known any better.

This time, I climbed the gate to her property. Jumping over it wasn't an option; I could barely stand straight. I shot the guards, just like before, though perhaps with a bit more malice in my heart.

I made my way to her room, killing anything that got in my way. Elizabeth waited there, just as she was forced to with this being a memory and all. I nearly raised my gun and shot without getting into our conversation as the memory dictated. But I didn't.

Because my memories didn't need to dictate anything.

They weren't permanent.

I slowly put my gun on the desk that stood between us.

"Miss Storey, you know why I'm here," I said. She nodded. "Good, cause this isn't the first time we've done this."

She arched an eyebrow at me, confused. She didn't lower her gun.

"I've already killed you. You're already dead." I held out my hands to placate her and keep the questions from falling out of her mouth. "Quite honestly, I don't care if you understand or not. I'm too tired to care. Too old." I gestured to the chair opposite her. "Care if I sit down?"

"Go ahead... um... I don't know your name."

"Jericho Falls," I said, sitting down with a grunt of pain. "I'm going to ask you a simple question. Do you want to die?"

"No. But I don't see that I have a choice."

"Right," I nodded. "That may be true. But don't you think that maybe if you kill me, you could get a few more days to live? Doesn't that just sound tremendously appealing?"

"Someone will just come and kill me later."

"Maybe," I said. I was thinking on what Savannah was screaming before she left my place. "But if I know anything about crossroads demons, it's that they do have to stick to their contracts. Your contract says you die today, correct?"

She nodded again, this time the barest flicker of hope showing in her eyes.

"Alright," I said. "So what if you don't die? What if that makes your contract invalid?"

"You're playing a 'what if' game with my life."

"You may get a chance to live," I said. I was so tired. Of everything. "Or I can kill you and guarantee you don't live. Which sounds better?"

She just stared at me for a long time. "Why are you doing this?"

"Cause I'm tired of reliving nightmares."

She nodded, as if she understood exactly what I meant.

"I need you to do something, though," I said. I'd made up my mind.

"OK?"

"Pick up your gun and shoot me. But don't miss. Don't let me live."

I'll give it to her, Elizabeth was a tough woman. Sure her hand trembled as she picked up the gun, but she *did* pick up the gun. "I don't know that I can actually shoot someone..."

"Do it," I said sitting up straighter and leaning forward. "Do it or I'll kill you and be on my way."

"But—"

"I'm going to count to three, and then I'm going to grab my gun there on the desk, and shoot you in the head. I won't miss. You will die."

"Look, I can't just—"

"One."

She got the message then. I saw it register on her face. She knew I'd do it. I admired her, more than a little. She would have been the kind of woman to get to know better.

"Two."

She lifted the gun, and pointed it straight at me. I started edging my hand towards my own weapon to force her hand. Just in case.

If my dreams—my nightmares—weren't permanent, and could be rewritten, then would my death let Elizabeth Storey live? For every seemingly good person like her, would every monster I'd killed come back to life too?

It didn't matter.

Monsters could always be killed by someone else.

But lives could rarely be brought back for a second chance.

I never got to "three."

Her gun went off, and I felt a lance of hot pain and fire tear through my throat. I fell backwards, gurgling on my blood. I would have preferred a clean, one-shot kill, but it was hard to be picky. I lay there, on Elizabeth's floor, my life flowing out of me. It didn't scare me. It felt familiar, like I was finishing off the story that was put on hold all those years ago in the cross-roads.

Elizabeth came into focus above me, gun pointed down. She couldn't miss at this range. Her eyes told a tale of gratitude and sorrow. I nodded at her.

Maybe Elizabeth Storey would live a good life. Maybe not. I was pretty sure I was about to die, here in this memory. But who can say what will really happen?

All I knew was that, for once, I was glad to have a dream I wouldn't survive.

She pulled the trigger.

THE DAMNATION OF ST. TERESA OF AVILA

Marie Brennan

They were on the road from Burgos to Alba de Tormes when she fell ill. The men who escorted her were careful not to mutter where she could hear; they knew she would chide them for it. She had suffered worse than the rain which poured down on them unceasing, worse than an archbishop who summoned an old woman miles across Spain and then turned her away. She had endured excommunication, the Inquisition, and sixty-seven years of life. This was merely the latest and least of her trials.

But they did mutter where she could not hear. They were not as holy as she, not as generous of spirit. They resented her ill treatment when it was merely an insult; when her brow heated and she began to cough, they did more than resent it. In low voices they blamed the archbishop and the noblewoman who called for the most revered of nuns to attend her in child-bed. The infant was already born when they arrived; once again, she had been brought all this way for nothing.

Not for nothing: that was what she would have said, if she knew of their complaints. God brought her here for a purpose.

God brought her here to die.

She was too ill to be moved, burning up with fever. By the night of October 4th, they knew her end was near. Her last words, whispered to her confessor, were: "My Lord, it is time to move on. Well then, may your will be done. O my Lord and my Spouse, the hour that I have longed for has come. It is time to meet one another."

She was dead come the following morning: October 15th, *anno Domini* 1582.

The night of her death lasted for ten days.

Not since the great illness of her youth has she known such suffering.

Fever permeates her body like a stain, seeping into every fiber of her being. She cannot move her limbs without pain, cannot swallow without agony, cannot even draw breath without that gentle movement jarring her head and making her vision swim. Lying prostrate in her narrow bed, she floats on a sea of fire. The recollection comes to her dimly of a holy man she had admired very much—she cannot recollect his name through the haze—whose response to great cold was to take off his cloak and open the door and window of his tiny cell. He did this, he told her, so that his body might enjoy the meagre increase of warmth when he closed the portals once more. She would emulate him if she could, but she cannot think how she might increase the heat from which she suffers. Perhaps there is a fireplace in the room?

It is foolish of her to lie in bed thus, and so to neglect her duties to God. Has she not learned again and again the futility of giving comfort to her body? She has never fared better than when she ignored her physical well-being and turned her thoughts only to the Sacred Humanity, whose suffering was so much greater than her own.

Despite her resolution to bear this cross with fortitude, a cry escapes her lips when she rolls over in her bed. Her arms shake like reeds in the wind as she tries to push herself upright—tries, and fails. Instead she slips her legs over the edge of the bed and slides until her knees strike the stone below. She cannot rise to look for a fireplace, for wood to burn and increase the heat, but this will do. There by the bed she does not need—his name was Peter of Alcantara, she remembers, and he slept upright with his head pillowed on a beam of wood—she kneels and folds her hands in prayer. Her body settles into this accustomed position with the familiarity of decades. She will not fall, unless God sees fit to grace her with His transformative presence. And that is not a thing she can bring about of her own effort or will. She must wait in humility, and turn her thoughts to Heaven.

For a day and a night she prays, her body shaking with the fire of lethal fever, wracked by torment she embraces with joy.

On the second day a servant comes to her, bearing food and drink. The woman exclaims in distress to see the nun out of bed, kneeling in obedience to God, and urges her to rest. "The Lord cannot doubt your devotion, after so many years," she says, trying to lift the dying woman from her place on the unforgiving stone.

The nun laughs at her. It is a thin, reedy sound, her voice worn almost to nothing by the fever. "Oh no, my child. It is a wonder that God should bestow any graces at all upon one so wicked as I. Time and time again He has shown me His favor, and time and time again I have turned away from it to dissipate myself in trivial pastimes. I have met many who are more deserving of such gifts than I am. How can I spurn Him again, when His generosity is so boundless?"

"You are not wicked," the serving-woman says. "You are the holiest nun in Spain. Even the greatest men of the Church acknowledge your worthiness."

"I have committed many sins for which I deserve hell. It is no credit to me that anyone should think well of me, for it means only that I have deceived them by hiding my great wickedness—which is another act for which I should repent."

The serving-woman stares at her in disbelief. "It is not so! There are wicked men and women in the world, but you are not counted among them. You do no justice to yourself, nor to any other, by weighing your own sins so heavily."

She cannot be made to rise from her knees. The serving-woman instead nods to the tray laid on a table and says, "Will you not at least take sustenance? You must fortify yourself, for the road ahead is long, and you must walk to its end."

But the nun smiles at her and says, "I would do better to feast upon the stale bread and bitter herbs of my own faults, than to feed myself in luxury. Peter of Alcantara ate but once every three days; it was very easy, he said, for those who accustom themselves to it."

And upon her words there is a bowl in her hands, filled with the rankest foul matter. From this she eats, choking on every bite, and then returns to her prayer.

On the third day she attains a measure of grace: the prayer of quiet.

In this state she is still capable of thought, and so she chides herself for conceiving of the moment as an achievement. She has achieved nothing. She is capable of nothing. Her actions are as nothing compared with the power of the Lord. Though she labors with great effort to bring her spirit closer to God, she cannot do one hundredth as well as her beloved Father in Heaven, without whom nothing is possible.

The prayer of quiet does not free her from the awareness of her dying body. The pain in her knees is excruciating, from hours pressed against the unforgiving stone. She trembles in every limb, caught between the heat of fever and the chill of the air, and sweat pours down her body to soak her robes. But she welcomes her suffering with open arms, knowing it is a gift from God. He is present with her now, separate but at her side, as a friend might sit nearby in silent companionship.

How much better is this, O Lord, than the worthless friendships with which she filled her youth! Once she squandered much of her time and thought on frivolous matters, which in those days seemed a source of pleasure to her, for she had no awareness of their cost to her soul. Now she knows those things, which once seemed so sweet, are poison compared to this: to sit in company with God, her thoughts bent wholly to sacred matters.

If His Majesty is merciful and kind, He will carry her yet further before He is done.

Even partial union with the divine cannot last forever. The next day she is alone once more, and grieves for the loss of holy companionship. When the door opens she turns away from it, not wishing to speak with the serving-woman again. She misses the solitude and silence of the cloister, which she labored for many years to restore after it fell into worldliness and distraction.

But the voice that comes from behind her is too deep for a woman—and familiar, though she has not heard it for many a year.

"My daughter."

There is grief in his voice, and love. Her thoughts should be bent entirely upon God, but against her better judgment she turns to look. In the doorway stands her father, in the prime of his life, younger than she is now. Sorrow lines his mouth and eyes as he looks upon her, weakened, dying.

The sight shakes her to the bone. "Father," she whispers, with lips cracked and bleeding from the dryness of the air. "Why are you here?"

He kneels with her, takes her trembling hands in his. Strong palms, broad, in which her own skeletal fingers look as fragile as winter twigs. "My poor daughter," he says, full of compassion. "Only you, in all the world, are caught in such a manner."

She wraps her fingers around the edges of his hands. The impulse is in her to take strength from his presence; she shakes it off. "What do you mean?"

"In your dying moments you turned your thoughts to God, and so you are caught outside of time. In the world from which you are departing, a great change is occurring. The drift of days and years have taken Easter from its proper place in the seasons, and so by command of His Holiness, Pope Gregory XIII, the calendar must be put right. Ten days shall never be —except for you.

"My daughter, you are transfixed upon the point of death; and there you must remain until those days have run their course." She can see the tears lining his eyes, shining gold in the light of the fire that never needs tending. "It grieves me to see you afflicted thus."

She shakes her head, and the world dances like a mirage. "I have neither need nor wish to accept your grief. Often have I bent my thoughts to the agony of our Savior upon the Cross, the scourging which preceded it. I have mortified my own flesh so as to share in His suffering, bloodying myself with a lash upon my own back. But for many years now I have felt as if I lived in a dream, taking little sense of pleasure or pain from anything which may happen to me. It is a great joy to be permitted to feel this torment."

Her words wrack her father. He releases her hands and reaches as if to embrace her, but she spurns it with an upraised hand. He says, "This torment may be inevitable, but it is not a thing in which to rejoice."

"How can it not be?" Her smile is beatific. "It is a gift from His Majesty, who plunges me into the depths of suffering so I may better know His love."

Her father shakes his head. "My daughter, my daughter... that is not the love of the Lord."

"I know no other," she says, and returns to her prayer.

On the following day, she enters a state of ecstasy, the second stage of prayer.

Her soul is swept up in familiar bonds, to which she submits with joy. Who would refuse to be the prisoner of Him whom she loves? Her limbs are no longer hers to move, and memory fades in the face of the overwhelming presence of God. She could, by great effort, bestir herself from this glorious union; she could direct her thoughts to her worthless flesh, cease her prayer and rise from her knees. But why would she? Nothing she could do in life or in the lingering moment of her death would equal the merit of this experience. And so she remains, transfixed like a moth upon a pin of red-hot iron.

There was a time when she refused this state. Her confessors feared it was a delusion sent by Satan, not a gift from God, and so they urged her away from it. The more they urged, the more frequently it came upon her, in defiance not only of their orders but of her own desire to bend to their will. Now there is none to obey but the Lord, and she is helpless before His might. Tears stream down her face, a waterfall without end, as she relinquishes all to His Majesty. In the depths of her soul she wishes for more, and despises herself for that wish, for she knows she is not worthy even of so much as this.

This sin, like all the others, she lays before God, and knows she does not deserve His forgiveness.

When the priest enters the next day, she wants to curse him, for upon his arrival her ecstasy ends.

"My child," he says, and his words recall her to herself. They echo her earthly father, as this man is her spiritual; she does not remember her father leaving. But only the two of them, nun and priest, are in the room now. "We must speak."

To him she does owe obedience, and so she struggles to rise. Her legs will not support her; spikes of pain thrust up through her body when she tries, so great she cannot even cry out. The priest aids her, lifting her to her feet and holding her there as her knees slowly grind straight.

"Your piety does you great credit," he says, "but you need not carry it so far. Our Father in Heaven is merciful and forgiving. He does not demand devotion beyond human endurance."

Her voice is thin and gasping, a mere ghost of itself. "I will endure any pain in His name."

"But you need not do so." He lowers her to the edge of the bed, but she will not lie down when he urges. "My child, it is no sin to rest. Your suffering will soon be done."

"I pray it is not so." Whether the sounds that comes from her mouth is a laugh or a sob, even she could not say. "When I am without His presence, I am dead; only in suffering for Him do I live."

The priest's face becomes stern. "You speak of things you do not truly understand. I tell you that you are in error, and you argue?"

She turns her face to the wall. "I have had confessors—I will not name them—who assured me that certain actions were no sin at all, when I know them to be venial, and that others were venial sins which are more rightly judged mortal. I am obedient to my spiritual director, even when he tells me to spurn God's presence, to spit upon Jesus when He comes; I have done this knowing that God will forgive me, for my obedience is correct, even if the direction I have received is wrong. But you are not my spiritual director."

"But what," he says, "if you have been advised wrongly again? St. Ignatius feared he had sinned when he trod upon two sticks of straw that had fallen in the shape of a cross. He saw in time that this was mere scrupulosity, not a true awareness of sin. What if God is not so strict as you believe, His judgment not so harsh?"

She bows her head, clasps her hands in her lap. "I have no power to confront my sin, no ability to overcome it. Only His Majesty can do so. All I may hope for is to subject myself utterly to His will, and pray."

The priest is gone. Biting down on a whimper, she leaves her bed to kneel upon the stone once more.

The memory comes to her that she wrote once of a moment much like this. In describing the third degree of prayer, the experience of ecstatic union, she said it was "like a dying man with the candle in his hand, on the point of dying the death desired."

How else is she to describe her state now? She is a dying woman, with the candle of her faith in her hand; she is suspended upon the point of death. She cannot ask for a greater trial or a greater blessing than this. The agony she feels as she rises into the third stage is the agony of bliss too great to bear; she is wholly caught up in the presence of God, incapable of freeing herself from it even if she desired. There is no freedom to be found outside this ecstatic suffering, only the bondage of separation from His Majesty.

Words spill senseless from her tongue, beyond her power to order or understand. She babbles of her joy, begs God to cut her flesh and spirit into pieces, so that she may have the honor and the delight of enduring them for her Lord. Once, when she was a young girl, she desired to be martyred for her faith, and ran away from home to seek death at the hands of the Moors. She knew nothing then of martyrdom. Those who have died for the glory of Heaven have done but little; the strength by which they endured was the strength of their Father, and not their own. That strength overtakes her now, imprisons her, subjects her to sweetness that sears as hot iron.

And so passes the seventh day.

The pain vanishes in a blaze of light, one that sears her eyes like cool fire.

When her vision clears, a radiant figure stands before her. Its naked flesh is without mark, androgynous, in shape like a human and yet not. The light behind it is a suggestion of wings.

"Glory be to God in the highest," it says. The voice rings upon her ears, a carillon of bells, a blast of horns, deafening in its softness.

She prostrates herself upon the stone, not daring to look upon the angel.

"Rise," it says, both gentle entreaty and command. "You have refused the kindnesses we offered to you in previous guises, and so we come to you now in our true form. If you will not heed a friendly servant, a father, a priest, then heed *us*."

She lifts herself to her knees. The pain has returned, but in lesser form: the mere pain of dying, and not the sweet agony of God's presence. To be alone, even when in the presence of an angel, leaves her more desolate than any fleshly torment.

It is also a warning.

The words of the radiant figure roll like thunder through the room. "God does not desire your suffering. You bring it upon yourself, and call it a gift of the Lord. You spurn the true gifts He has given you: your intelligence you dismiss as foolishness, your strength of will you abandon as weakness. He gives you free will to choose virtue or sin, but you cast your virtues onto the dung-heap and declare yourself powerless to confront sin. Your humility is so great as to become arrogance."

That terrible voice stops, and silence falls. Then, more quietly, it asks, "What have you to say?"

She fixes her gaze upon the floor, refusing to gaze upon that light. "When I was in my youth," she says, "and began to experience visions of God, the priests around me were sore afraid. They believed my visions to be no true gift from Heaven, but a delusion sent by Satan, meant to lure me into damnation."

"They were no thing of Satan."

On that point they agree. She says, "I have feared this myself many times over the years, for I know I am a woman, and vulnerable to such fancies. But this reassurance I have: I know that Satan would not attempt to lure me into good behavior, but would only encourage me toward sin. Therefore, if what my visions advised ran counter to what I knew of God's will, I would heed them not. I say *if*, for it did not occur. The visions were true."

Now, at last, she raises her eyes, confronting the creature before her directly. "Until now."

The wings shift and flare.

"You are no angel," she says, "but a false vision sent by the Devil. At this, the moment of my death, you hope to entrap me with soft words of kindness. His Majesty would not advise me so. And here is my proof: that He is not with me when you come."

A mere whisper from the creature is still enough to shake her bones. "I come to bring you God's mercy—which you have ever refused to accept."

She folds her hands in prayer, turns her attention to Heaven. And the light fades away, leaving a whisper of sorrow in its wake.

* * *

The cruelest torment she suffers is this: the awareness that she is not yet dead.

She does not wish to die so that her agony may end. If it went on for a hundred nights, she would praise the Lord. But so long as she lives, she is in the world, and is apart from His Majesty. How is such loneliness to be endured?

She cannot even think of it. God sweeps her up into the transformative union of prayer, the fourth and highest water; she is incapable of anything. Her tongue is silent, her body still. She cannot feel the stone beneath her shoulder where she has fallen, nor the fever that burns her from within, convulsing her limbs. Had she the ability to speak, to think, to will anything beyond that which His Majesty chooses to inflict, she would beg Him to pour this precious liquor into a more worthy vessel, shower His graces upon one who would do good with them instead of casting them into the mire. But the Lord, in His wisdom, chooses to show to her the depths of her worthlessness, by bringing her into the perfection of His self.

It could be an eternity. It comes near to being so. But as it always has before, the moment ends, and she is cast once more out into the world.

On the tenth day she is alone. Not even the false angel comes to visit her, in any guise.

She remembers her life, from its early, foolish days through her attempts to follow wisdom. How many hours and days did she squander in reading tales of knights! How much breath did she waste in conversation with friends, with kin, when she could have been speaking praise for the Lord! And how much joy came to her when she moved, however slowly, with however many stumbles, toward the truth: that to know God's love is to suffer.

Slowly, because of the weakness of her body, she stretches herself out upon the stone, lying prostrate. It may have been a lie of Satan that her suffering is to last for ten days, as the world outside moves to right its calculation of time. She does not know. But either way, she will be prepared.

"Lord," she whispers to the stone, "either let me suffer, or let me die."

Words she has said many times before. Now, though, they are the purest expression of her faith.

And God answers her prayer.

She feels the agony of His presence coming upon her. With her last strength, she turns onto her back, facing Heaven.

The seraph descends, as it did once before, so many years before. In its hand it holds a golden spear with a fiery point, which it thrusts deep into her heart, penetrating her entrails. When the spear withdraws, all thought, all awareness vanish, burned to nothing in the blaze of perfect suffering.

When the morning came, they found her cold and quiet in her bed, the sheets about her soaked with sweat.

Her passing was an occasion of great mourning, for she had been a leader to many; and also of joy, for surely now she was with God. The word "saint" was on the lips of many before the month was out. Not even thirty-two years passed before she was beatified; not even forty altogether before she was canonized. All the Catholic world knew of St. Teresa of Ávila, whose wisdom and holiness were a model to all.

But of this the saint knew nothing. She remains forever at the point of death: caught in the Hell she made for herself, and welcomed with tears of joy.

MAN IN THE MIDDLE

Max Gladstone

The old man behind the reception desk sat as still as a sculpture of bone and meat and skin. Tara set down the books she carried and extended her hand. "Hi. I'm Ms. Abernathy, the new tenant in 17-B."

He did not respond.

"I'm moving into my office today." The lobby doors opened behind her to admit the swamp air of Alt Coulumb summer, and a box-laden cart pushed by a skinny tonsured man in deep red robes. A cigarette jutted proudly from Abelard's mouth. "A bit behind schedule," she said. "I have more stuff than I thought."

Abelard tried to stop the cart, and mostly succeeded. One box teetering on the corner toppled to the floor, and the many scaly bony somethings inside hissed. He scrambled to right the box before the somethings escaped.

Tara ignored them. "Do you have a freight lift?"

No answer. The old man's eyes were amber and flat as coins. Tara blinked and examined him for Craft, but the lobby was bare of sorcery aside from security and air conditioning wards. The old man was neither debt-zombie nor illusion. She rang the bell on the desk. "Hello?"

A short, dark-haired woman in a bottle-green jacket emerged from behind a smoked glass door marked FACILITIES, her weapons-grade smile on full beam. "Oh! Ms. Abernathy, I'm so sorry, I was just in the other room, Gabby Shearstone, building management, so pleased to meet you, the rental office said you'd drop by," all in a single breath. "I'm so sorry, I just had to,

I mean, very pleased to meet you, I hope Robert hasn't been any trouble."

"'Trouble' isn't what I'd call it."

"Oh, yes." Shearstone crossed behind the desk and set a hand on the old man's shoulder. "He's been with the building forever, real stalwart, bit long-toothed, that's all. Watches out for us, sort of a good luck charm." One corner of Robert's mouth may have tilted up a fraction of a centimeter. Then again, maybe not. "Do you need help with your things?"

Abelard had levered the fallen box back into position with no harm done. Well—not much. A single whip-thin tentacle of segmented bone slipped out of the box's side to snare his wrist, needle-spines pressing in.

"I think we'll be fine," she said, "if you can just show us to the lift."

"It's a nice enough office," Abelard said once they'd dealt with the tentacle and unloaded the cart. "If you like that sort of thing."

"Nice enough?" Tara spread her arms wide and turned a slow circle without touching the walls. "It's great. I'll set my desk right here."

"Back to the window?"

"Have you ever tried to work facing a view like that?" Temple Green ranged to the south: a vast and verdant lawn landscaped with wards. In its center rose the eighty-story temple of Kos Everburning, a bonfire of black stone that shamed the skyscrapers at the Green's edge. Cloud obscured the Temple's summit, but somewhere up there the fire god's flame burned. She could see it with her eyes closed.

Abelard shrugged, and sat on a pile of boxes—shook them first, though, to ensure nothing inside was alive or a reasonable facsimile thereof. He took another drag on his cigarette. Tara, as ever, resisted asking him to put it out. No accounting for religious observance. "They don't give us a ton of windows down in the boiler room."

"So you know what I mean. Plus, this way the light will fall on my work rather than in my eyes."

"Reading in direct sunlight makes you go blind, I hear."

"I thought that was reading in the dark."

He took a small silver box from his tool belt, and ashed his cigarette within. "There's more than enough office space in the temple. Just ask the Cardinals."

"We've gone over this," Tara said. "You need a Craftswoman in-house to work sorcery and skullduggery for you. I'm happy to have the position. But I'm not a theist, and proximity to gods can warp unbelieving minds; there's a gravitational effect, inverse-square law sort of thing. Also, I'd like to keep a door open to private and pro bono clients—get to know the city that way."

"You could meet them in the temple."

"Sure. Because the first thing people want to do when they have problems is run to confess them before God."

Abelard blinked. "Well. Yes?"

She smiled in disbelief at Abelard and his Church. Gods were outmoded and oppressive technology, which human Craft made obsolete—*just keep telling yourself that*—but Kos Everburning did attract loyal people.

As well as the other kind.

"Look," she said, "it's not as if I'll be off church property. You still own this building."

"What if we need your help? Should I start training for the hundred?"

"More like the four hundred. No. That's what this is for." She shoved him in the shoulder. "Scoot off that box." He obeyed, with a mock bow that swept his robes behind him.

She traced an opening sigil on the box. The rings glyphed into her fore-finger glowed, and box-top tongues unlaced themselves to reveal inky dark-ness within. She reached into that dark, clenched her teeth at the unpleasant squeak of packing immaterial on skin, and lifted a gleaming brass machine from the black.

"What is it?"

"Nightmare telegraph terminal," she said. "Colberg-Arendt model C. Demonglass-toothed gears, reclaimed brass fittings, obsidian palimpsest knife, seven-dimensional clockspring, adjustable soul draw." She set the ma-chine on the floor and sat cross-legged before it. Bone keys gleamed hun-grily beneath their varnish, and the ball-hammer hovered over blood-red ribbon. "The Cardinals will see this in the Craftwork department's operat-ing budget, by the way."

"You have an operating budget?"

She ignored the question. "It's the best option. Paired quills need prop-erly trained scribes; we could use watches, but for some reason the Church doesn't like to use professional dreamers for transmission and processing."

"It's the screams, I think."

"That's what gags are for," she said. "Anyway, this avoids the problem. The paired machine's back in Maintenance. I showed Sister Muriel how to use it yesterday."

"Paired how?"

She tapped the bell jar nestled beneath the keys. A knot of gray matter floated there, suspended in bubbling amber fluid. "Rat brain. One here, one back at Muriel's, entangled via nightmare. I type, the terminal translates what I've typed through the brain into nightmare, and it comes out the other end."

"That's sick."

"We wouldn't have to do this," she said, "if Alt Coulumb used rat post like a sensible city. Look, it works perfectly." Tara bent over the keyboard and typed, one finger at a time so he could see: HELLO MURIEL. HOW ARE YOU? "Now we just wait for her to see the message and—"

The terminal screamed a scream of nails and knives and too little grease. Gears scuttled. Lightning crackled in recessed tubes. Amber fluid bubbled faster as the brain within convulsed. The ball-hammer struck ribbon and parchment with the sickening sound of nails pounded into flesh.

OOOAZX$%KKKK877332332MAKETHESCREAMSTOP

Ash drifted from Abelard's cigarette to the carpet. "Is that supposed to happen?"

She ignored him, or tried to. MURIEL, DO YOU COPY?

The carriage revolved and again the machine thrilled to life or something like it.

SEVENSUNSRISEOVERDESSICATEDPLAINTHEPYRAMIDBURNS
THEWATCHERSWITHINTWISTANDSCREAMTHEYKILLGODSTHE
REDONTTHEY

"No," she said. "Unless Muriel's having a very bad day."

Sister Muriel's days were never bad as such; sometimes, though, they were interesting, and what a woman in charge of maintaining the boilers and power couplings that illuminated six million people's nights called "interesting," others might term catastrophic. Fortunately, when Tara and Abelard reached the maintenance office at the temple core a hard-run several minutes later, they found her engrossed by an enormous scroll of divine circuitry. She tapped her foot to the beat of bellows and the clank of gears that issued from the black hole in the floor. "Ms. Abernathy! An unexpected surprise. And Abelard—where have you been keeping yourself recently?"

He shrunk within his robes. "I've been busy."

"Sister Muriel," Tara said, once she recovered her breath. "Did you get a message from me an hour ago?"

"In fact I did. Quite confusing. It's on the counter by the teakettle."

Tara picked her way around tables piled with charts and reference books, and found the piece of parchment tented face-down. That only puzzled her until she read the words written on the scrap. She wouldn't want them coming into contact with a work surface either, let alone a place where people prepared their tea. The Kathic alphabet and mathematical symbol set weren't well suited to Abyssal dialects, but the nightmare telegraph had made a copyist's best effort. "It printed this?"

"Sixty-three minutes ago," Muriel said without looking up, "to judge by the big clock."

"There isn't a clock here."

"There is. You can feel it in the floor."

"The vibrations," Abelard explained. "They change throughout the day."

"This isn't what I sent." Tara didn't offer to translate. The acts described were maddening, literally.

"As I thought," Muriel said. "A shame. Those devices would be terribly useful if we could ever make them work."

"You've tried to install a telegraph before?"

"A decade or so back. Never could get anything through, and the operators kept going insane. Same reason we don't use dreamers in the temple."

"You didn't think to mention this when I showed up with a new model?"

Muriel set down her pen and adjusted her glasses. "I assumed they'd solved the problem."

"But the devices worked when I tried them here yesterday."

"There never was a problem communicating *within* the temple—only with sending messages outside its walls."

"How long has this been a problem?"

"Since the Wars at least."

"And in fifty years no one ever investigated why they don't work?"

Muriel raised her eyes toward where the sky would have been if not for several dozen floors of intervening temple. "We didn't need them. Lord Kos binds His faithful into communion. I am certain He would accept you, if you sought Him."

"I'm sure," she said, and slid the paper into her pocket.

"It's not a bad idea," Abelard said later, back among the boxes. "If you join the Church, even as a lay sister, Lord Kos will bind you to the community when you're needed. All are one in faith."

"Do you have any idea how creepy that sounds?"

"Says the woman burning a pentagram into the carpet."

"It's not a pentagram." Tara carved Abyssal letters into the shag with the blade of her knife. Reality bled briefly, then scabbed over, leaving a soft green glow behind. Three more cuts, and a long curve for which she really ought to have used a compass. No worries—she didn't plan this ward to last long. "Not to sound ungrateful, but I've thrown my lot in with the Church enough for one lifetime. I left a good job to work here. I made the right decision. But I don't want to pretend to be something I'm not. And I'm a Craftswoman. I have no faith."

"You do," he said, "whether you realize it or not."

"Again: creepy." She stood and sheathed her blade. "There we go. It's time."

"Time for what?"

The circle burned green, and the shadows it cast grew deeper, spreading and joining into black.

"Tara?"

"Time," she said, "for debugging."

"Do you know what you're doing?"

She drew a black candle from her purse, cut ten minutes' length, set the stub in a shallow dish inside the circle and lit the wick with a snap of her fingers. "Not exactly. But there's a first time for everything."

She closed her eyes and fell back and out through the holes in her skull. The nightmare wasn't hard to find; she'd visited it every night for months, since her first mad days in Alt Coulumb. Held motionless as an oil slick tickled across her cheek to press against her lips and no matter how she clenched her jaw still it forced itself through and down her throat and the world transformed to silver and the sky to a goddess smiling down and she was loved and loved back only she was screaming too and somewhere a dead man laughed—

Deeper down, past the drowning, past the love, past worship and bliss and the obliteration of the self, past the moment of the mind overshadowed, through waving green fronds and shining clouds and distant screams as the world took her apart.

She fell through the central terror of the race, consumed and buried, drowning and owned, toward the final base truth of her death. Nightmares whirled through crimson seas. A globe of stars surrounded her, and every star screamed.

Not many people slept this afternoon in Alt Coulumb: night shift workers mostly, and children at school. She heard distant cries in foreign tongues. Far to the east, in the Skeld Archipelago, Kavekanese beachcombers tossed in holocaust visions. And beyond, further east, always east, the continental terrors of Iskar and the Gleb burned.

She did not need them now.

She hung in the center of the fear, and in that dark place intoned the serial name of her nightmare telegraph. Somewhere far away, the Craft circle in which her physical body slept erupted with unholy light, as did the smaller circle she'd drawn around the telegraph. She hoped Abelard was sitting down.

One of the many holes in the sky swelled, another world terrible and white beyond: the shared nightmare in which the firm of Colberg and Arendt had trapped the two rat-minds. The light caught her, and she landed kneeling on white stone.

Solid ground underfoot; alabaster walls towered to her either side, and the white flat sky above glowed with soft ghostlight. Ahead, other halls split off at right angles. Behind, no paths diverged: distance crunched the hallway to a perspective point. As she watched, though, the walls drew together, or the hallway extended, or—no. The perspective itself was approaching, the point that bound all others into itself. It prowled forth, hungry.

So that's the game, Tara thought. *Find the center, which will lead to the other rat, to the other maze.*

Then she ran.

She sprinted down the hall, turned a sharp right, then right again, then left, past two intersections and then the second left.

Then she looked back over her shoulder and saw a single straight hallway without twists or turns, and the perspective-point drawn closer.

Dammit.

Mazes. Follow the same wall to find the center. Assuming rat brains' nightmare mazes obey topological law, which obviously this—

She ignored herself. Left left straight left, left at the fork, u-turn, left again and straight, fast as her fear could take her, pulse live in her throat. The other mind was here somewhere. Shared terror should draw them inexorably together. Not inexorably enough, though. Not as inexorably as the crushing point which slid still nearer.

Her mind chattered sorcerous solutions: fly above the maze, shatter the walls with your will, arrest time, call upon the rats who have died here to guide you. No, no, and twice no again. Craftwork was will, bargain, imposition, control. To assert control here was to deny the nightmare. This was the human mind flayed naked, helpless.

Except this nightmare wasn't human, was it?

This was a rat's dream. Would a rat solve a maze like a woman? Researchers in the Hidden Schools studied the one to model the other, yes, but rats didn't know graph theory.

Not that Tara claimed to understand graph theory either—but that was beside the current point.

The rat's nightmare was not the maze, but the researcher at its end—the pleasant young woman in the lab coat with ether-soaked rag and scalpel and university grant to study the effects of certain tree-bark powders on memory. The rat feared the moment its choices ran out.

She stopped running.

Behind her, the perspective point approached. She took a deep breath and ran toward it: the rest of her life, the straight path past all choices. And this wasn't just a ratty terror. She felt it, too: her commitment to Abelard's church, to Alt Coulumb, rejecting her old life for a new career, the thrill of possibility that might be just the knife's thrill at her throat. And she heard, she was, the scuttling of claws over stone, and felt a smaller but no less earnest brain echo her fear as the vanishing point leapt forward and the world's lines crushed her and she was—

through—

but not into another maze, nor into another rat.

She broke to a thousand shards caught in a whirlwind of flame. Howls consumed her, and in faceted vision she saw a priest devoured by her parishioners, a temple and a city burning, immense stone monsters clawing buildings down, granite-fanged mouths descending to rend bared sweaty throats. Tossed by wind she traced her fractured landscape: a tower built of nightmares, and around it a broad flat plane littered with impaled human beings.

And beyond all that, composed by the intersection of the screams, a man's voice repeated over and over:

Hello hello does anyone receive Code Blue Code Blue cut off behind enemy lines request extraction repeat request extraction hello—

She tried to pull herself together but the mind in its terror held her fast and she spun clutching bare broken memories for purchase until she guttered like a candle flame and—

Woke, in her box-filled office, with sunset red through the window and Abelard watching.

She sat up, eyes wide, and sat in her suit on the carpet for a while, breathing herself back into her skin. Her eyes did not need to adjust to the dimmer room; she'd come from a much darker place. The candle lay by her right hand. Three minutes' burn remained, but the fire was out. "What happened?"

Abelard didn't answer at first. "Wherever you were, it didn't sound good. You were—I put out the candle." He held up a soot-streaked thumb and forefinger. "I'm sorry. Was I wrong?"

In her seven minutes' unconsciousness a family of small insects must have crawled into her mouth, died, and decayed. "In the abstract," she said, "yes. But I don't know what three more minutes in there would have done to me. Thank you."

He looked away fast. "Did you find the rat dream?"

"That, and something else. Something big, and hungry, and old."

"A demon?"

"Demons don't dream like that," she said. "How long has the Church owned this building?"

"We built it," he said. "Part of our expansion planning back at the turn of the last century. Rented all the units early on, since the priesthood wasn't big enough for the space. The plan was to move lower-rank cells and clerical offices here piecemeal. When the God Wars came we gave up on that idea, and good thing too—we bring in so much office rent it's embarrassing."

"And that warding circle on Temple Green wasn't built until the end of the God Wars."

He took a long slow drag through his cigarette, and she didn't blame him. It was a bald question on a sensitive subject. "No," he said. "The warding circle was the Cardinal's secret. He used acolytes and contractors for heavy lifting, but only for isolated sections of the work. Nobody knew the shape of the whole project."

She nodded.

"Tara, what's going on?"

"I need a drink," she said. "And an ambulance."

Recessed ghostlights did not protect the building's lobby against the gathering dusk. Outside, rush hour thronged the streets with driverless carriages and golem wagons and pedestrians. Glass doors muted all sound, but let the shadows in.

Robert sat behind the front desk, silent and still.

Tara drew her work knife and cut small wounds in the air, rays pointing toward an invisible circle of which the old man was the center. Abelard stood well clear of the silver glow and the darkness that adhered to Tara's coat. As night descended and stars came out, her power grew. "You think he's the problem with your machine?"

She heard, and ignored, his skepticism. "Not him as he is now. What he used to be." She worked faster, brow furrowed, trying to recall the precise curves she needed, the cues and invocation language. "Alt Coulumb was neutral back in the God Wars, and its neutrality was important. If you had joined the Wars, the siege of Alt Selene might have turned out differently, and if that broke the other way, the entire eastern theater looks... bad. For us. For Craftswomen and Craftsmen, I mean."

"What does that have to do with your infernal device breaking down?"

She drew the eighth ray pointing inward, and added summoning clauses in vertical chains. "The Craftsmen cared which way Alt Coulumb jumped. It's hard to infiltrate a priesthood without getting sucked in, but someone might have found an edge case—a position inside the Church's borders that didn't involve worship or oaths of fealty or anything dangerous like that. A night watchman's position, say, or a receptionist's. That's ideal: long late stretches with nothing to do, during which our agent could leave his body on autopilot and dream himself into priests' nightmares, taste your fears, strain them for insight and intelligence. Until, one night while our spy was on patrol, the Cardinal completed his warding circle—trapping our itinerant dreamer in. Where he bloated, consuming terror until he occupied so much local dreamspace not even a simple transmission could pass through with-out being broken by his mind."

Abelard took a slow step back.

"The ambulance should be here in a few minutes," he said.

"Might as well start," she said. "I don't want to waste their time."

She drew a needle of light from the burning symbols she'd drawn, leaned over the desk, and touched it, lightly, to the center of the old man's forehead.

Somewhere, a heavy door opened.

Somewhere, a sixty-year scream fell silent.

Somewhere, an enormous hand closed around a fistful of broken glass.

In the lobby, Robert's open eyes opened again, and burned black. His bared shadow-fangs tripped poison. Lightning webbed his body; glyphs long-dormant, camouflaged with the care and expense of fine military Craft, burned beaconfires beneath his skin.

Tara wondered, briefly, whether her excitement at this turn of events indi-cated some deep-seated psychological problem. Then she filed that thought for later review.

"Passphrase," he said, in a voice of doom unused for forty years.

"The war's over," she said. "We won."

Madness glittered in those black-on-black eyes. "Passphrase."

"You were trapped behind a ward, in nightmares. You're not thinking clearly. That body's been dormant for forty years. We'll fix you, but we need to get you to a hospital now."

He inhaled, a slower, deeper breath than his body had drawn in four decades. He turned from her to scan the lobby—and saw Abelard. Saw, rather, a priest. The enemy.

His eyes tightened.

She intercepted the shadow-spear before it skewered Abelard, broke it to shards on the shield of her will. The effort staggered her, and her vision grayed. She wasn't kitted out for war, and the old man was. "You don't understand. The war's over."

"Wars," he said, "never end. Only traitors claim otherwise."

"Listen to me, dammit."

But he wasn't—there were chattering voices inside his head, nightmares layered, forty years of secrets compressed into a single skull. The skin of the world warped, and multicolored strange-pupiled eyes peered in.

She drew her knife, and bared her teeth.

A door opened behind her, and a familiar voice said: "Bob?"

The thing in Robert's skin turned, and Tara drew back: Shearstone, the building manager, stood by the door to her office, one hand on the knob, mouth open, uncomprehending. "What's going on here?"

Nightmare shadows sharpened to flensing scythes. Tara raised her knife—

And then the black eyes closed, and the shadows closed with them. The old man settled to the floor. When his eyelids fluttered open the irises within were amber once more. A tongue flicked out, and the night watchman said, "Gabby?"

Then he collapsed.

Far away, a siren wailed.

Abelard stood with Tara on the sidewalk and watched the ambulance pull back from the curb. He lit a cigarette from its predecessor's ember. "You're not—what he said."

"No." She crossed her arms. "But that's what I look like to him."

"No wonder you don't want offices in the tower. You're scared of being on the wrong side."

"I'm not scared of anything," she said, and he didn't argue. "There aren't any sides in this. Not the way he thinks."

"What's wrong, then?"

"Just—him. Stuck in your church for years, mad and alone. If he could have connected, someone might have saved him. But he had nothing to draw on but other peoples' nightmares." She shook her head. "I should unpack. See you tomorrow."

"I, um."

She paused at the door.

"Some of the technicians, I mean, we play cards on Fourthdays. Lightweight stuff, you know, for fun. Maybe you'd like to come sometime?"

"You won't mind losing to a godless witch?"

"You won't mind losing to ignorant god-botherers?"

She grinned. "You're on. And thanks."

"For what?" He saluted her as if his cigarette were a rapier. "Good night. Pleasant dreams."

"To both of us," she said.

U.I.

Howard Tayler

She looks like one of Sedgwick's neo-fey things, you know? Reptilian humanoid, digitigrade legs, smooth scales like a snake, and just as sexy as those elves that Wilson designed. Lithe, graceful, and dressed in a white half-tee and skin-tight black compression shorts. Oh, and she's got a knife in one hand. Anyway, she's brand new, and disturbingly hawt so I totally forget to throw a wardstone. I whip my Mossberg up, and sure enough, the reptilian fey-lady is on top of me before I can fire.

My Turtleskin vest stops her knife, but she's shoved the Mossberg aside where it's useless. I pull the trigger anyway, and the shotgun's report is an explosion just a foot away from my face. Hers, too, lucky me. Repto-elf leaps away from me, screaming, and I see she's bleeding from one of her ears.

I pump the shotgun and snug it up into my shoulder. Now that I've got the barrel pointing in the right direction I can't miss. And just as I'm putting the bead on that scaly bitch something punches me in the back. Something hot.

A spear point, shimmering with magical fire, bursts out of my chest. A stick of butter would have made better body armor. My hands go numb almost instantly, but I don't drop the Mossberg. I can still squeeze off a shot, and maybe I'll get lucky. There's a trauma phial in my pocket and—

Whatever's holding the spear lifts me off the ground with it and shakes me. The shotgun goes flying, my coat is whipping up around my face, and I think I've got my own arterial blood splashing up into my nose. Then I hit the asphalt, and the rough, blood-spattered pavement is all I can focus on before everything goes dark.

"*Totally killed me, man. And yeah, it was intense.*"

"*I bet. Anyway, congratulations. You're dreaming the game. Now the real work begins. Did you write it up?*"

"*Not yet. I'm more used to writing up defects.*"

"*This isn't a defect, obviously. Log this in Q-Case, and tell the story. And be sure to include as much detail as you can on that reptilian fey chick.*"

"*You like my design?*"

"*Actually, I want to run it past Sedgwick and see if he's already built something like it.*"

"*Oh. That makes sense. I probably caught a glimpse of that in an image library, and then inserted it into my dream.*"

"*Right. Most importantly, though, before you head home this evening, get the latest build of the Player's Quest Log onto your tablet, and then take the tablet with you to bed.*"

"*...*"

"*Seriously. Put it on the nightstand. Now that you're dreaming the game, you need to log these things the moment you wake up.*"

"*Oh. Right. No problem.*"

I used to wonder why they'd put an old-fashioned cube farm in a video game. Sure, it's retro, but not in a good way. People played these games to get *out* of the cube farms, right? Well, I'm running through a cube farm now, and I totally get it. Wish fulfillment. We don't just want to escape the cubes. We want to transform them, and nothing transforms fabric-walled office cubes like a flamethrower.

Talk about immersion. I can feel the heat of the flames on my face. I can feel the heat reflecting off the glass. Heat's good, too. There's no way one of those hopped up frog-elves is going to survive *this* towering infer—

No way! The frelf comes right through the wall of fire! I point the nozzle at him, splashing burning naphtha all over him but he doesn't slow. He's covered in some protective gel.

The flamethrower takes both hands, which is why I popped a wardstone in my mouth before I lit up. Good thing, too. I spit it right in front of me, and Burning Kermit slams into an invisible wall just an arm's length from my throat.

I snuff the flamethrower and holster the nozzle, freeing up one hand for my .45. The greased frog-elf trails patches of burning oil as he hops around to my left, looking for the edge of the ward. I shuffle back, checking my six as I raise the Glock. I can't shoot through the wardwall, but unlike this burning, amphibious fey, I can see exactly where the edge is.

He's past that edge before he realizes I've got the pistol up, so I put two in his chest, and one in his wide, froggy head. That's how it's done. I turn and run for the far end of the cube farm. Gotta get out of here before the flames catch up with me. I'm hustling past sad little desks dressed with family photos and houseplants when I hear shots.

I duck and weave, and try to dive into one of those cubbies of human misery, but something hits me in the back and pushes me down. No pain, though. The bullet must have—

Suddenly I'm on fire. Some freaking frog-fey marksman managed to shoot through a wall of flames and hit the tank on my back. You know what'd be nice right now? One of those ice-phials, but that's DLC, and I'm pretty sure I can't download DLC into my dream.

"It only took four days for my kids to get mad at me."

"What's the matter?"

"And I quote: 'WE can't take video games to bed, but DADDY gets to play on his tablet in the middle of the night.'"

"Sorry about that. If it's any consolation, now that you're on the Deep UI team for Streets of Fey, we're paying you for sleeping."

"Yeah?"

"One-eighth time, since that's about as long as you'll spend logging things, but yeah."

"Well, tonight I'm turning the volume down on the tablet. The Player Quest Log says I recorded three dreams last night, even though I only remember the last one."

"That's common with dream journaling. Once you start logging dreams, your subconscious figures out that they're important to you. You start waking

up at the end of each dream, but you'll only really be awake enough to write down what happened."

"That's creepy."

"Psychology 101 stuff. Creepy, but true."

"'Kay. I guess I'll transfer the PQL stuff into Q-Case, and buy myself an extra dessert to celebrate the pay bump."

"One more thing before dessert: the server logs say that you used your DLC account last night."

"Really? I'll have to check the quest log. I didn't see that in there."

"You might not have put it in the log, but the server says you picked up the Elemental Phials download."

"Holy shit. In one of the dreams my flame tank got hit, and I died on fire. I remember really wishing I had a Phial of Ice on me."

"Outstanding. Make sure to include that detail when you write this up. We'll cross-link it to everything you play-tested during the last couple of days."

"Right. Hey, can I ask you an over-my-pay-grade question?"

"You can ask."

"Is that what all those frame-rate tweaks, and low-frequency audio tracks are for? Getting people to buy DLC in their sleep?"

"Let's just say that you should hang on to those options you've got."

I'm cutting through the city cemetery, which isn't something I'd do if this was a zombie game, but it's not a zombie game. I don't need to worry about my ankle getting grabbed by something busting out of the ground, and this is a newer cemetery with flat, ground-level grave stones. Lots of open space, which is good for me because I'm running a shooter build. The only places things can jump out at me is from behind the trees, and there's plenty of space between them.

Well, except for those three up ahead, near the gate. If I were going to hide behind a tree and ambush a Fey-Hunter, that's the spot I'd pick. And now that I've seen it, I don't have any problem approaching from the side instead of straight in, making it much harder for even the sneakiest fey to stay hidden.

From the side I can see that it's clear, but I hear some creaking above me. Monkey-fey, perhaps? Haven't seen those yet. Maybe—

The whole tree uproots itself from the ground, and reshapes itself with a cacophony of creaking, kind of like if a Transformer started out as a tree and then did that *murp-voom-murp-murp-voom* thing and turned into this big, wooden troll.

The troll is at least three times my height. The root ball has swung up to form a head, and the thickest parts of the trunk are now its torso and legs. The arms are formed from thick branches, and the clawed hands are each the size of a car tire. All the skinny branches and leaves have bunched together behind the torso, so that as the troll hunches down and knuckle-walks toward me there's sort of a foliage-finned stegosaurus look to it.

Enough admiration. I swing my carbine up and squeeze off a burst. Some bark peels back, but these .223 rounds obviously won't do lumberjack shit against a troll made out of tree-trunk.

That bundle of foliage coming off its back gives me an idea. I've got the Elemental Phials DLC, and at least one of these little bottles of juicy magic will work as a fireball. I backpedal and check my six while feeling around in my coat pocket for the phial I want. Helpfully, it's hot to the touch. I pull the phial up to my face, bite the cork off, and whisper "burn, baby, burn" into the mouth of the bottle.

Then I throw it.

Hucking an actual bottle of flammable liquid is kind of a dicey proposition, I imagine. Throwing a magic phial of fire is simple and effective, because magic. The fireball centers itself on the troll, and expands to almost the full size of the monster. Sure enough, the foliage on its back catches, and as the fireball goes out, the troll's entire backside is ablaze, a concentrated crown-fire destroying what I hope are vital bits.

The troll roars in pain, staggers, and then drops. I smile as a watch the writhing pile of wood burn.

That *morp-voom-voom* transformation sounds a couple of times behind me, and then twice more right in front of me as the remaining two trees at the cemetery's gate rip themselves out of the ground. I don't have any more of that fireball-in-a-bottle, and even if I did, it sounds like I'd need at least four bottles.

Maybe this encounter is designed to sap the player's resources. Maybe, though, there's another solution.

* * *

"Honey, are you okay?"

"Shh. Trolls. Gotta tool up."

"You need to wake up."

"I am awake. Don't worry. I'll be back out in just a sec."

Bam. Transmutation Wards DLC, right here. Just what I needed.

The four giant wooden trolls have surrounded me, but are keeping a bit of distance. They don't want me setting two fires with one bottle. It's too bad that's not what I have planned for them.

I pull my shiny new wardstone from my pocket, blow a kiss at it, and drop it at my feet. "Surround me and be flesh," I whisper.

One of the trolls charges, and when he's about thirty feet away he staggers a bit. There's a ripping noise, and then all those hard, wooden bits are made of deep, brown flesh. I cut loose with the carbine, and this time it does real damage. The troll howls in a voice that sounds much more human than it used to, and then it falls backward, the finger-thin flesh and bones of its fin shattering in a wretched mess as it hits.

I smile and turn to face the closest of the remaining three.

"If you hurry this up, I might get to see if the meat you turn into is any good cooked over that fire."

"It says here you pulled DLC in the middle of the night, again."

"Oh, it's better than that. My quest log says I grabbed the DLC during the dream because I needed it for a troll fight."

"Trunk-trolls?"

"Yeah. The big wooden dudes. Fire phial will take 'em out one at a time, but the wood-to-flesh wardstone softened all of them up enough for me to take 'em out with the .223."

"Nice. You've logged all this?"

"I have. I... um... I also made a note of the dressing-down Sarah gave me. I told her about the stock options, and she likes the promise of financial security, but right now she's not happy about being woken up at 2:00 am by me tapping out log entries on my tablet."

"Ha! There might be some 'compatibility issues' with ubiquitous immersion

and real-life friends and family."

"Ubiquitous Immersion?"

"Yeah. 'U.I.' Did you think that U.I. still stood for 'User Interface?'"

I'm standing over the steaming corpses of over a dozen frog-fey. A pride of bone jackals is rattling at me as they circle at the edge of the street lamp's glow, but they're not going to attack. I've got a pocket full of bones-to-dust wardstones, and I think these skeletal hounds can smell the threat. Also, they don't want a fight. They want to eat fresh frog.

I may have leveled this shooter of mine as far as I can. It feels weird to say that in a dream, but that's not half so weird as having my dream be a continuation of the online play. And even that isn't as weird as lucidly considering this, but not being able to just log out and wake up. Or wake up and log out.

I'm feeling hungry, and I have zero interest in frog legs, so I walk down the middle of the empty street toward Fernando's Diner. Fernando serves this neat blend of Tex-Mex and Mom-and-Pop diner fare that I wish existed outside the game. I'm pretty sure the design team put it in here just so they could have menus that say "meatloaf relleno" and "cherry churro pie," but their silliness sounds really tasty right now.

"Daddy? Are you making breakfast? It's still dark out."

"Breakfast menu served 24 hours."

"What menu?"

"Sorry. I handed it back to Fernando. I'm having the hashbrown tacos."

"It looks like you're just cooking eggs."

"I'm not the cook here, sweetie."

"Mom? MOM! Dad's using the stove. I think he's asleep."

"I'm wide awake, little one. Just hungry. Had to dance around a lot in that last fight. Damn frogs got pretty close."

Yeah, that totally hit the spot. I wipe my face clean, and drop a ten on the counter.

"Fernando?" I call out. "Settling up!"

Fernando doesn't answer. I peer around the end of the counter into the kitchen, but he's not there, either. He must have stepped into the walk-in fridge.

Suddenly he stands, as if he'd been lying down behind the counter.

"There you are. Ten-spot's right there next to your ha—"

Fernando opens his mouth, and keeps opening it until his jaw is all the way down on the top of his spattered apron. Row after row of shark teeth all angle back to a pulsing pink throat that looks too far back to be part of Fernando.

I jump back and reach for my pistol. Not-Fernando's jaw keeps dropping until his "mouth" extends from just below his nose all the way down to his crotch. His clothes slide out of the way and change colors, turning pink, grey, and a couple of shades of green. Some sort of shape-shifting mouth-monster?

I fire, and the creature doesn't even flinch. I wonder if it's smiling at me as it leaps, and then I'm inside the mouth and a thousand teeth are stabbing me at once.

"Shape-shifting shark-fey? Really?"

"Scared the crap out of me. Totally killed me, too. Surprising, since I haven't had a game death in a while now. My shooter is maxed out."

"Maybe it's time to take a break, then. Focus on build management for a couple of weeks."

"Aww. I was hoping to try a brawl-and-blade character build."

"Yeah… according to PQL, you've put in 31 hours of game play here at the office just in the last week."

"Sorry. Is that too much?"

"Scenario testing and use-case generation should make up less than 25% of your work day. The other 75% goes into documentation, interaction with team members, and various kinds of overhead."

"Oh. Damn. I thought I was taking care of all that stuff."

"You are. I mean, you've missed a couple of team meetings, but we're square on the productivity side. Everything you're testing is getting documented. Vilkus over in Dev is singing your praises."

"Cool. I'm glad it's useful. I bet my knives-and-knuckles run will be even better."

"Okay, look. I gotta say no. PQL says that last week, in addition to your in-office time, you put in 82 hours of game play while you were asleep. That's almost twelve hours per night."

"Not possible. I'm in bed at ten, and up at five-thirty."

"PQL measures this using the logged events of the dreams as a yardstick, so there might be time compression going on, but you're still covering a hell of a lot of game play while you're asleep."

"Isn't that what we want?"

"Sure, sure. But we think that maybe the next piece you should test is NOT playing."

"Well… crap. That sounds kind of boring."

"Take a little time to write about being bored then. Another use case. And yes, build management is kind of dull, but if you need to scratch the gaming itch, you can take some company time to play one of those PopCrap mini games. Bejunkled, or maybe that old one with the garden and the zombies."

"If I end up sorting garbage by color during my sleep, you're going to hear about it."

"We're paying you to tell us."

I'm standing in the kitchen of a suburban home, and the wind is roaring outside in the night. Holy shit, this is cool. I'm starting this new character build from the dream platform rather than online. This is completely off the hook. Also, screw *Bejunkled*. I don't want to end up addicted to some mindless puzzler where the prize is recyclable aluminum. I'm a fey hunter, not a dumpster diver.

I decided on a brawler, right? Oh, and blades. I look around the kitchen. This one does NOT have a massive meat-cleaver hanging conveniently on a hook in the corner. Of course it doesn't. That'd be too easy. I start opening drawers, and the steak knives are in the first drawer I check. I guess that makes sense. At least some of the level design in here is coming out of my head, and that's the drawer where we keep the steak knives back in the real world.

Which means… YES! The knife block with the good vegetable knife is tucked back behind the bread machine. I draw the vegetable knife from the block, and there's this tingling feeling, like I'm Arthur pulling the sword from the stone or something. Oh, yeah. That's the DING of completing the first tutorial quest and arming the character.

There's a creaking from the trees outside. I hope that's just the wind, because as a 1st-level knives-and-knuckles brawler I stand exactly zero chance against a wood troll. I kill the kitchen lights and let my eyes adjust before moving to the window.

The two trees in the front yard are small, like the homeowner just put 'em in a couple of years ago. Tract-home trees. Not big enough to make that creaking I'm hearing.

There's an oak in the back, and while the ends of the top branches are whipping around in the wind, it hasn't turned into a troll yet. This might just be house noise.

A scream jolts me out of my stupid sense of security. It's a woman's scream, coming from upstairs. Knife at the ready, I run up the short flight to the upper floor of the split-level house, and I'm almost at the top when I trip.

I'd forgotten how clumsy a 1st-level character is. I go down on one knee, splaying both hands out in front of me, and of course I lose the knife. It tumbles along the carpeted hall and stops halfway to the open door where a twenty-something woman in pajama pants and a tee shirt stands wide-eyed.

"Wake up, for God's sake!"

"I'm awake. I'm fine. What's the matter?"

"You're the matter!"

"You threw a knife at me! Not cool. You weren't supposed to have figured it out already."

The woman opens her mouth as if to scream again, but there's no sound beyond the hiss of exhalation as her jaw drops to her navel.

No time to think about it. I run, bending low and scooping up the knife. Maybe I can kill this shape-shifting suburbanite before she swallows me whole. I lunge and thrust with the knife and the shifter blocks with a pillow. I try to push through it, but the knife isn't that sharp, and this bitch is strong. She shoves the pillow sideways and I lose the knife again as it tumbles to the carpet.

A pillow. First-level brawler gets foiled by a pillow? I guess maxing out a shooter unlocked legendary mode.

Her maw hasn't opened any further, so I take a chance and throw a punch at her nose, right above the uppermost row of shark teeth.

"Daddy! Stop!"

"Run! This isn't your mother! It—"

It stumbles into the wall, and I'm clear to snatch the knife off the floor. I grab it and lunge again, and the shifter throws its arms up in defense. I cut it good, maybe hitting an artery in the wrist because there's blood every-where now. The shifter screams, and it must be a magical defense because I fumble the knife a third time trying to adjust my grip.

Or maybe first-level characters really suck.

The shifter has backed into the master bedroom and put the bed between it and me. It's bleeding, but I'm not sure I can actually take it. Besides, I'll get more XP if I save the innocent kids.

"Come with me! Outside!"

"No! You can't—"

"—make us! You're sleepwalking! You hit Mommy, and you have bloody—"

No time to argue. I throw the kids under arms, run outside. Damn, they're heavy, and I run like a fat guy. Legendary mode is going to suck, and I'm not going to mince words when I write this up. I'm low-level, unarmed, and I'm already up against shapeshifters?

I drop the kids on the lawn, and they run away from me and away from the house. Good instincts. They're quick, and they even get all the way past those tiny tract-home trees before one of them wakes up and transforms into a skinny version of the wood troll.

This I might be able to take with my bare hands. I grab it before it can reach out for the fleeing kids, and I bend the slender branch all the way back and down. The wood is green, but I can hear it splintering, and the twig-troll turns on me with a reedy scream and its one good arm. I grab that one, and wrestle with the monster.

Damn, but it's tough. I feel like an idiot when, after what has to be five minutes of twisting and wrenching, I'm finally able to bend another branch far enough to break it. The troll shudders and goes still. I shudder, too, with a tingling chill that announces more quest completion.

The first quest can't really be complete, though. Not with the shapeshifter still at large in that house. I turn back to the house, see the shapeshifter peering through the window next to the front door. She's holding something up to her face.

Headlights approach from the end of this sleepy little street. It's a police cruiser. The fey never drove cars before, so I'm reasonably confident that these police are on my side. I wait in the yard. The cruiser pulls right up to the curb, and two officers step out.

"Evening, sir. It's a little late for gardening, wouldn't you say?"

"I'm—"

The cop's jaw drops to his chest. I scream, because if the cop is a shape-shifting fey, legendary mode is about to kick my ass all the way to the curb, and then curb-stomp me for good measure.

"Sir, settle down."

I lunge, slamming my shoulder into him before he can go full shark-mouth. He's reaching for his weapon, but I saw that coming, and I know how to play a shooter. I grab and twist, and now I've got something I know how to fight with.

As a player anyway. Let's see how good a shot this low-level knives-and-knuckles loser is. I pull the gun close to me and step backward, firing as I go. The cop doubles over and tumbles back against his cruiser. There's movement at the house, so I turn and put three rounds through the window, aiming at a silhouette that I hope was the suburban sharkfey shifter.

That shadow drops almost instantly, a good sign that I tagged center-of-mass. Yeah, I know how to use a gun. Maybe I'll go back to the brawling after I've leveled up a few times and acquired some boosts.

Something slams into my side, and takes me down. Shit, I forgot about the other cop. And I don't have that level 3 duster with the Turtleskin lining yet. God, this hurts. Legendary sucks hard and out loud, and I'm kissing the street. Maybe... maybe I can grab some DLC. A healing phial, or a lifegiver. Probably need the lifegiver by the time I get back.

Assuming I can even wake up before this stupid character dies.

THE QUALITY OF LIGHT IS NOT STRAIN'D

Peter Orullian

It's morning. Before dawn. You like to get to the lake early, when its surface is a broad mirror. Glassy smooth. The air is chill, but you like that, too. It feels like anticipation. A whole new day is ahead. And you enjoy the way the lake fogs appear and eventually lift when the sun hits the cold water.

You find your spot on the bank of the small, remote lake. No reeds here to tangle your fishing line. And you've had good luck here before. Carefully, you thread a worm onto your fishhook. But before you cast, the early morning stillness breaks. Footsteps on the old dock. Less than a good cast from here.

No one comes to this lake. This spot.

A cry echoes out across the lake. A loon?

Quietly, you sit up and peer over the reeds. In morning's half-light you see the shape of a man walking the weathered boards of the dock. Slow steps. In oiled workboots. The dock groans. Rusty nails creak. The water ripples outward in tiny waves. Disturbing the glazed water.

The man carries no pole. And the dock is old. Very old. No boat or canoe is tethered there. But the man does have something in his arms.

And your eight-year-old heart begins to pound in your chest.

You would run from here, but the man would hear you.

So, you stay. And watch. And wait...

* * *

John leaned against the front of his '72 Ford F250 and looked east toward dawn. Still a few minutes away. From the cab, his Clarion deck played a guitar song after a baroque fashion. He had some Linkin Park in the truck. Some funk, too. But not here. Not *his* spot. Far from the crowds. High on a long plain of sage. He'd come to relax, to await sunrise. A whole new day ahead.

He traced the aureate rim across the mountains east and the fade of blue toward violet above him. The air was mild, windless. The ground smelled wet with dew. A renewing scent. He came to this secluded spot to be alone. To take in the patient, uncomplicated way of things he only seemed to find here. To get away from mid-terms—art and music double major. And to burn away images that crept up from sleep.

Casting his gaze around, he started at the sudden sight of a stooped figure standing thirty paces to his right and looking toward the same promise of dawn.

"Didn't think anyone else got up early enough to watch the old disk float up, huh?" the old man said, still facing east.

John said nothing, staring at the man in surprise. The old fellow's beard fell halfway down his chest, and his knees were crooked. Even from thirty paces away, the lines at the corners of the old man's eyes and mouth were deep furrows. His back had a soft bend as if he'd never been offered a seat. But his face had a patient, bland look to it. And the slope of his stance made John think of the comfortable way one reclines in a hammock.

The man chortled, cocking his head to one side in a combination gesture of disgust and bewilderment.

"You know, Johnny, it's precious few that actually see the sun come up." His eyes never left the brightest portion of the sky above the mountain crest he faced.

"All right, where'd you get my name? Is this a set-up? Did Kyle put you up to this—"

"Nah, it's on your license plate."

John pressed his lips together in an awkward moment of embarrassment. All of which faded at the sound of being called "Johnny," not "John" as his family and friends called him. As he'd insisted since middle school. Somehow that tail-end vowel always lent a shade of condescension to the name.

Or made him feel like a kid again. Small. Enough so that he'd spent the additional licensing fee for a personalized plate that read simply, "John."

"We're pretty far from the road. I didn't see your car on my way up." The spot was pretty removed, or so John had thought.

"Just watching the sunrise from *this* spot this morning," the man said, as if that should make things clear.

From the truck a harpsichord joined the guitar melody, and John nudged a rock with the toe of an aging Nike.

"This spot?"

"Well, yeah, always another spot, you see, and in each one the light..." He trailed off, the words becoming part of the flatland around them. He seemed to finish the thought in his head, lifting his woolly brows to punctuate its truth. He shifted his weight from one foot to the other and inhaled deeply. He held still, then blew the air out in a whoosh, leaving him looking more deflated than before.

"If I'm trespassing, mister, I'll leave." John nodded back toward the road.

"Quiet, it's ready to come."

John turned and watched as the sun burned a swath slowly into the morning sky. The mountain appeared as a birth mother, graciously, gracefully sending its young into the world. Light touched the tips of a few cedar trees, it gleamed on the chrome of John's bumper, the low brush grew tall shadows, and John watched it touch the old man's eyes. It held there brighter than any other place.

After the sun had cleared the mountain and then some, the old man turned toward him. John then saw something even more perplexing than the man's sudden appearance, more odd than his fixation on that single point east. The man looked in John's direction, over his shoulder, at his waist, at the trunk of the tree to his right and then perhaps somewhere near his eyes. They were the random eye movements of the blind.

"Are you—"

"Without the faculty of vision? Physically challenged, perhaps?" He began a sort of waddle toward John. "I've chosen something else for my eyes, John. An exchange, you might say."

John retreated a step, panic creeping into his chest. *Am I really afraid of an old bent man?* The hair on his neck rose as if to answer that.

"You're scared just now, John, but I'm not much in the way of a threat to you." Still, John removed his hands from his pockets. Just in case. The man took no note of it. "Beautiful again, wasn't it? Never a disappointment. Always a touch of the eternal there in those few seconds. I might just paint this one." The old guy, close now, leaned back against the front of John's truck and folded his arms against his sunken chest.

The worry of danger faded. The strangeness of this meeting was replaced by an irrepressible feeling of relief. Not relief that the man seemed friendly after all. No, John was relieved that he wasn't the only one. He'd always assumed there were others. But finding someone else who came to watch the sunrise. Just that. And alone.

He wondered if the old man came for the same reasons he did. Because it was another start. Because it could somehow bridge over the disappointments. "Things will look better in the morning," his mom used to say. Goddamn right.

Maybe the old guy was a pervert, a wacko. Or maybe he was a recluse or eccentric or part of an elaborate dream or rouse or whatever. But John found that he urgently wanted to say this thing inside him, a thing he'd felt deep for a long time. Maybe something he'd *kept* deep for a long time. It felt like a confession. John looked at the old man next to him. The curve in the guy's back, the folds at the corners of his eyes... they were like invitations.

The sun rode higher on the still morning sky. John looked at it and spoke softly, "I feel like I *have* to watch it."

The old guy looked at John and smiled the way a dad smiles at a son's first little league dinger. His eyes didn't quite find John's own, but the light there was friendly enough and John was glad he'd spoken.

"Glad to have watched the sun with you, Johnny."

John continued to watch Helios ride. Moments later when he again looked back to the space the old guy had occupied, the man was gone.

The dirt grinds beneath your boots. Chippewas, like your pa wore. Deeply worn. But newly oiled, to keep them soft.

The air gets a mite colder when you get to the old dock. Lake water gives off a chill. You pause a moment there before stepping onto the worn planks and starting for the end.

You used to fish here with your pa. Right from this dock. Out-of-the-way place. Small. Forgotten, maybe.

Reeds are growing up from between the dock planks, which are warped and bleached from years of sun. Reeds are deep green, though. Healthy. And the lake water is icy blue.

Your boots make a hollow thomp thomp as you walk slowly out onto the dock. With each step, your chest aches more. Aches with failure. Aches with your loss of faith.

Halfway out, the small bundle you've brought wrapped in your best flannel shirt... cries. Sounds like a loon echoing out over the still lake.

You stand there, comforting your child, rocking him in your arms. He gives you a sleepy face, and settles. It's early. And you want to be done before the sun comes up.

Secrets don't like the sun.

The park rang with the chatter, screams, and delight of children. Parents sat idly by, beneath the shade of large maple trees while kids postured, frolicked, and created worlds the adults had forgotten. The lawns were long and the sand beneath the monkey bars kicked and sprayed under the feet of tiny armies. John sat on a green Parks and Recreation bench with his sister Stephanie, keeping an eye on her older boy Mark.

"How are things with Marie?" Steph probed, stowing the remains of Mark's peanut butter and jelly sandwich in a sandwich baggie.

"They're okay." John tried to dodge, pointing at her son. "He's sure getting big."

"Listen, Mom really likes Marie. It'd sure be nice to have cousins." Steph nudged John with an elbow and barked a single laugh. John adored his only sister. She liked the Three Stooges, she used a pipe wrench better than anyone he knew, and she never meddled unless given a direct order by their mother.

Her ex-husband Taylor had left when Melissa, her second child, was born. John had known he would. It wasn't intuition, it was the conversation they'd had over a cold case of Natural Light and a Mets game on Taylor's big flat screen. *Men weren't meant to settle down,* Taylor had interjected during a standings recap. *Nature dictates it. Women seek out stability. Men must try to copulate as often as they can to ensure the survival of their genes in the gene pool. It's natural. It's scientific.*

Uh-huh, was all John had said, too astounded and too drunk to debate the finer points of human nature.

"I really like Marie, Steph, but I wouldn't be good for anybody right now." John had learned that phrase from a particularly good art film he'd seen at the Student Union. And as long as Steph made an effort, then a report could be shared with Mom and everyone was off the hook.

"Well, you should think about it. She—"

A wail cut Steph off. It belonged to Melissa. They both got to their feet and were across the lawn to the monkey bars in the space of four seconds.

"What happened?" Steph demanded of the cluster of children who stared down at Melissa lying prostrate on the sand.

"She didn't duck in time," Mark explained. He was in the second row of the cluster.

"Come here," Steph said in strident tones.

Mark parted the two boys in front of him and knelt next to his mother. Melissa was developing a large welt between her eyes and sobbed with the slow, trembling shakes of a child both hurt and embarrassed. John watched all this, yet remained intensely aware of the position of the sun, the heat it baked into his shoulders, and the mimicking shadow he threw to his right across the sand.

"Now tell me what happened." Steph was holding Mark's hand as if she might get more of the truth by making physical contact.

"I told you, she was running toward the monkey bars. We were playing spaceship, and we were about to blast off. She was trying to get on before we left her. She didn't duck and she ran into the low bar." Mark wouldn't have lied, not while his mother had a hand on him.

Melissa groaned and pulled her elbows back to prop herself up. Tears streamed from her eyes, seeming to be more a result of the blow to the bridge of her nose than of honest pain. She blinked and looked up toward her mother. But not at her, over her. An expression of wonder spread on Melissa's face.

"Hey, Mom, everything looks bright and sparkly."

"What, honey?" Steph released Mark who retreated back into the dissipating crowd.

"With tears in my eyes, everything looks like a big bright star."

At that, something stirred inside John. It was like the deep basso of a Wagner piece. Disturbing and unrelenting. Steph dried Melissa's tears and stood her up. The tragedy averted, the spaceship could finally take off.

Soft and warm. And the smell of soap. You feel and smell these things and know they are Daddy's shirt. You're in his arms. He's taking you for a walk like he sometimes does. But you don't know this path. These trees.

You hear his big boots below. It's still dark, but not too dark. Morning time will be soon.

Then Daddy's boots make a different noise. A not-on-the-ground noise. And it gets colder on your arms and cheeks.

You cry to let Daddy know. Your cry makes a far-away sound. Again and again you hear your cry. Daddy stops and whispers 'hush' and rocks you. He looks tired. His eyes have lines around them. So does his forehead. It looks like pain.

You feel sad for him. He has had this face a lot lately. But you have only had two birthdays. Your best help is to smile for him. Which you do.

You wish the daytime would come. Things are better then.

But Daddy doesn't wait for daytime. He keeps walking now. His big boots making that low strange not-the-ground noise.

And you see water.

John went to meet Kyle at the Henry Fellows Art Gallery the following Thursday. As he entered the doors he saw Ken Mailer standing at the top of the stairs in his uniform, looking bored and slightly aggravated. At the sight of John, Ken smiled and relaxed his stance.

"Hey, man, good to see you here as a paying customer." Ken grabbed John's hand and shook it firmly.

"Yeah, yeah. But, honestly, it was cool of you arrange a private showing for us last time."

Ken had let John and Kyle in one night after closing to walk the gallery at their leisure. The traveling artist being featured that time had been an un-known guy named Artanis. And Ken had joined them when he saw how much fun it could be. The lights were turned out at night, except for a few small security ceiling lamps. So Kyle had brought a couple of flashlights, and they'd taken turns spotlighting paintings and sculptures. The fun part was changing the proximity of the light to capture just parts of a painting, or angles on a sculpture that gave the piece new dimensions. Faces could be highlighted or effectively removed from a particular work. Sculptures might consist of specific body parts, or cast shadows of their own. By changing the focus of the flashlight, different parts of a piece of art became more important, others less so or not at all. Then it could all be reversed. It had been the best way John had ever seen art.

"No problem. In fact let's do it again." Ken straightened up as one of the gallery partners brushed by wearing a name badge.

"I'll be in touch," John said and nodded conspiratorially.

John then stepped into the hall proper. A few appraising glances flicked over him, finding him of no particular consequence and moving on. He smiled at that and spotted Kyle considering a large triptych in the corner. He began folding himself through the crowd. Snatches of conversation streamed by like lines from "The Love Song of J. Alfred Prufrock." But he gained ground relatively unscathed by the self-important critiques on the collection Mr. Fellows had assembled.

"Hey, thought you weren't going to make it," Kyle said, removing his Lennon-style spectacles to look through his worsening vision at the piece he was mooning over.

"Professor Pitrell said it was mandatory, right?" John looked back over the sophists milling about the gallery. "You know, I actually heard a woman pooh-pooh a painting by Diego Rivera," John mocked in a frivolous tone.

"Not really!" Kyle put back, joining the satire on crusty bunches who spend far too much time pretending to be vinophiles.

"Well, you know, it's simply unacceptable! You'd think they let just anyone scribble something to hang in a gallery. And my word, have you seen the people? I guess art is just going down the crapper."

Kyle laughed and John smiled.

"This is great, Johnny, check it out."

John turned to look at the triptych. That Wagner feeling swelled again deep inside.

"You okay? You look pale," Kyle said. The crowd was rallying on a large orange painting, one man explaining the piece and its use of negative space in ululating tones much like a carnival barker. John heard it all distantly. He was falling into the triptych.

The right panel was a gorgeous representation of dawn. The color was mute, unimportant in the chiaroscuro tradition. The elegance of the sun drawing heavenward over the mildness of an untouched landscaped was compelling. The panel was mostly dark, a line where the light of day had, and had not, reached falling on a slant downward, obscuring the world beneath in shadow. And somehow the painter had conveyed the feeling that all that was entombed in the dark but struggled toward the dawning.

The contrast was stark and yet the panel wanted the observer to feel a semblance of calm, of peacefulness.

The central panel did not.

It was larger than either side panel and was dominated by a small hillside town. Cobblestone streets curled and ended the way they seemed always to do. The entire scene was rustic but busy. Figures moved in a seventeenth-century market, carts and goods on display for buyers. At one end stood a man with a hand clutching for a bag being extended toward him. With is other hand, the man pointed toward a child cowering beneath the cart behind him. The child's entire body fell in the shade of the cart. Except for his hands. Splay-fingered, the boy's hands reached back toward his father, catching the light of day.

Below this, another street turned onto an alley where a beggar on his hands and knees bent over a bowl with a large crack in one side. The beggar had no shirt. Something about the beggar's exposed skin unsettled John. The recesses of the alley, the look of bared earth as something familiar to this thinning figure... all of it bore an ugliness John quickly turned away from.

To the left of these two scenes a woman moved through the streets with a sizable entourage in tow. She inclined her brow a bit, her left hand holding a fan. Her dress hung long and gave the impression of great weight. Yet, she walked unaided, and as if well-rehearsed for a pageant in which she might be the only performer. John then found the distortion: The shadow the woman threw was exaggerated and bloated to encompass her entire train.

The town was divided by the line begun in the right panel. Some of its people existed where the sun had arrived, some where the cold of night still held. It was here, in the dark bottom right-hand corner of the middle panel, that the jail stood. Dark-cloaked figures guarded it close. The jail had a big window with thick black bars, and behind them, nearly filling the window, was a set of eyes, distorted to several times their actual size.

The image troubled him.

Kyle was continuing with his satirical sketch on the artsy types milling about them. John wasn't listening. He was remembering the other chiaro-scuro paintings he'd seen. The art of light and dark had never for him been so punishing as this. This triptych had light in it, but that light only served to make the shadows darker.

He then remembered something the old man at the sunrise had said: *Precious few actually see the sun come up.*

John studied the eyes behind the bars. Then the child's hands trying to fold into the sunlight, the crack in the beggar's bowl, the obese shadow of the slender woman. And a scream began to mount behind his teeth. He closed his eyes against the images. And in those random patterns which shift on the inside of one's eyelids, he saw a single circle unmoving and bright.

He took a breath, then slowly opened his eyes. The left panel was almost entirely done in light tones. The city was gone, the world pristine and enve-loped in the rays of the sun two panels away. As John smelled the rich tones of wine, as heels clicked on art gallery tiles, a sour paste glued his mouth shut. There. A small, ever so small figure standing on a gentle slope near the edge of the left panel. John's eyes were watering now, and his vision became blurred. But he looked hard at the panel and decided the small figure was normal, perhaps a farmer, perhaps just a whim of the artist, before Kyle pulled him away toward a sculpture the carnival barker was spouting about.

Your fishing pole is forgotten as you watch the man take his last few steps to-ward the end of the dock. There are no reeds growing up through the dock-boards out there. Too deep.

The dock bobs a little more with each of the man's last steps. The glassy smooth lake now has just small ripples disturbing its mirror surface.

The sun is closer. Everything a bit brighter. You see the first wisps of lake fog that will come on full when the sun shines on the water.

The man kneels at the end of the dock near the tires nailed there. Bumpers for boats that no longer come to this place.

The man unwraps what he's carrying from a faded flannel shirt. That's when you see it. That's when you see the child. Maybe two years old. Maybe.

Your heart really starts to thump now. You don't know why. Your feelings don't feel like your own. More like they belong to this place, this moment, this man. And by God, you think you're seeing through the man's eyes as—

—You look down at your child and unwrap him from your best flannel. Shabby thing, really. But still your best. The child looks up at you with trusting eyes. That's the thing that hurts most, by God.

You pause. You can see the chill raising goosebumps on his fair skin. He's getting uncomfortable. You look up and around the whole lake. Small place. But peaceful. Smells like pine wet with dew. Wisps of lake fog just starting.

A few birds call, their voices echoing across the water. Grebes. Helldivers, they're called. And the water is brighter now with the nearness of sunup.

You should hurry.

You look around a last time. Nothing. No one. You didn't expect there would be. Not here. And not early like this. Except...

You have the strange sensation of seeing yourself from the bank a stone's throw away, of being in the head of someone else...

"He knew what?" Marie asked.

John stared back a long moment. "He knew my name."

The old man looked blind, John thought, *but then how did he see my name on my license plate?*

John sat at the kitchen table, staring endlessly at a half of grapefruit Marie had sliced for him. He had meant not to come here. He had meant definitely not to tell Marie anything about the old man, the painting, or the dreams and memories that seemed to be waking inside him. He didn't want to place useless baggage on her. He didn't want useless baggage.

Yet John had done just that. Told her.

Marie was flushing the toilet down the hall, bathroom door open. His love for her was precisely because she *was* so open, so practical, so matter-of-fact. She always said the thing that spoke most clearly to the problem he was having. When there'd been trouble at work, she'd said, "Quit." When his dog of sixteen years was having trouble standing, she'd said, "Put her to sleep." When he couldn't decide whether to pursue the relationship with her any longer, she'd said, "Fuck me." Kyle had told John he thought her heart was cast iron, but that she had a great ass. John thought she was what women were like after they had seen a man walking naked to pick up his socks.

He lifted his gaze from the grapefruit as Marie came down the hall. Her top pants button was undone and she wore only a bra above her waist.

"I thought you said you were tired, that it might have been a dream." She began loading the dishwasher.

"Maybe, but now I'm not so sure." John's voice was weak as it sounded off the Formica. *Maybe I just ought to eat my grapefruit*, he thought obtusely.

"Do you think this guy might be after you?"

John silently thanked Marie for conceding the reality of the man at sunrise. He also knew she was eliminating possibilities, narrowing the parameters so that John could put this behind him, behind them.

"No," John said, "I don't think he's after me."

"Did he say anything threatening?"

"No, he just talked about the sun." John understood that she was having him say these things so that hearing himself say them would end his uncertainty. He also knew that if he continued with the current topic that it would escalate into a fight. Marie was good about listening, but only as long as she felt discussion was useful.

Marie turned toward John, wiping her hands on a dish towel.

"Listen, if the guy was there at all he didn't do anything wrong, didn't appear to want to hurt you. Just don't go back to that spot to watch the sun rise again. And if it keeps you up nights, call in a description of him to the police." Her tone made an end of the conversation.

John nodded.

"Now come in here." She walked down the hall, past the bathroom, into her bedroom.

John left the grapefruit untouched on the table. He followed her into the room and found her lying on the bed. She wasn't writhing with expectant passion, she simply lay there looking beautiful and at ease. John saw himself across the room in her dresser mirror and noted the rise in his pants. He did in fact want to be with her. He could let himself be close to her, say things he didn't have courage to say any other time. He even decided their talk had perhaps helped him. The old man had been friendly, why should he worry about it? One bad dream, or one odd acquaintance. He pulled off his shirt and lay down beside her.

As with every time they made love, Marie initiated everything. She pulled down his jeans, she positioned herself atop him. She kissed him deeply, then rose up to a sitting posture. John's one request was always that they make love with the light on. He never told her that it wasn't because he wanted to be able to see her. It was because the light somehow validated their love.

She began to rock slowly back and forth on top of him. John closed his eyes and moved in complimenting waves.

"I love you," John said, and a smile found the corner of his lip.

"I love you, too, John." Marie paused. "And I want you to give me a child."

John's eyes startled wide. He looked up to see Marie's face, to see if she was serious, to see if she was smiling. But he couldn't see her face. Marie's head fell directly between John's eyes and the overhead light. It was only a dim sixty-watt bulb mounted behind a frosted glass fixture, but the effect was to blacken Marie's head in a silhouette. The fringes of her hair were like a dim corona.

"Did you hear me? I want a child. I want us to have a baby." Marie's voice seemed earnest, creative, sharing, but the words were dark for John. They echoed down a dark well into his memory and threatened to disturb things he'd spent a lifetime covering over.

That Wagner feeling again. Panic. A warning feeling.

Her face was a shadow, her head obscuring the only source of light in the room. Wildly he wondered if she was doing it deliberately. Her head was like an eclipse, and that seemed to be the most condemning, the most fearful thing of all. At that moment, he slipped out of her. He didn't need to see her face to know what it looked like now. But he didn't care. She still blocked the light. She still cast a shadow on him. He needed to see those sixty watts.

"You son of a bitch," she whispered.

John bobbed his head side to side in an effort to see the light, and was unable. Her arms had locked on his own and she was tightening her grip.

Please, he screamed in his mind, *just get up and then you can do whatever you want. Kick me in the balls, whatever, just please get off!*

Marie slapped him viciously. Twice. John struggled to free himself, his fear irrational and growing. He felt weak, as if he'd been hamstrung. He began to have hate in him for Marie, she didn't have the right to block the light.

Then she crawled off him, weeping. She sat at the edge of the bed with her face in her hands, crying. John wanted to feel for her, but all he felt was incredible relief at being able to see that bulb again. That light fixture with two or three dead flies in it. That light with a crack along its right side, near a screw.

"Get out," Marie said softly, then rose. "Just get out."

She walked out. John then allowed the expression of relief to run free on his face. Later he might feel the weight of this moment. Right now he only wanted to stare at the bulb. It was glorious to see. Nothing like the sun, but it shone its comfort for him, and he appreciated it.

As you watch, the man looks at you from the end of the dock. Or at least it seems like he's looking at you. You're looking through dense reeds here. He can't really see you. But for a moment it's like you can see him and see yourself through his eyes at the same time

And you get the feeling you should hurry. But all you're doing is watching. And feeling worried and scared and guilty.

The man pulls something from the deep back pocket of his overalls. Looks like a thick roll of tape. Then from his other back pocket he pulls something else. You can't tell what it is. He sets both these things on the dock next to the child.

You almost cry out then. Almost. Partly to tell him that whatever he's planning to do, stop. Just stop. And partly because now you're looking up at the man's careworn face, a few days of beard. It's a bit disorienting. Like you're laying on the dock and—

You feel cold again. Colder. The warm and soft is gone. The floor beneath you is hard. You smell the water now, but you can't see it anymore.

Daddy is looking down at you. His sad won't go away. Your smile didn't work. Daddies are that way, sometimes. They carry heavy things. Heavy for their arms. And heavy inside.

So, you try not to cry about the cold. Or the hard beneath you. You try to be still, as Daddy gets things from his pockets. Daddy has something to do, you can tell. Your best help is to not make it harder for him. Mommy has taught you that. And you love Daddy, so you will try.

You can tell the sun is almost up, too. Things will be better when it comes. Things feel better. Brighter.

Until then, you can be still.

When John got home he didn't have the energy to sleep. He drew a glass of room-temperature water from the faucet and walked to the living room. It was late and he could see the sallow orange shadows cast by a street lamp across the his dusty wood floor. That wouldn't do. He turned on the lamp and collapsed into a large rocker. He pulled the afghan off the backrest and wrapped it around his shoulders.

The room wasn't well decorated. An old piano which suffered dismal attempts every holiday season to reproduce Christmas carols. A magazine bin, an unused fireplace tools set, an antiquated Zenith TV. John stared at the lifeless screen and rocked. It was his mind that needed the rest, he decided, not his body, and for the moment, staring at a blank TV screen seemed to do nicely. The room smelled the way a room does when only one lamp is burning. And the sounds he heard were those high-pitched squeals you only hear when it's quiet.

He took a swallow from his glass and wiped away the water mustache. He lifted the glass and looked at the lamp through the water. Water bent the light, if he remembered the physics. The glass bent the image. His face reflected in the glass looked distended and freakish. "Things will look better in the morning," he told himself, and smiled without much humor.

John rested his head on the high back of the rocker and began pushing with his feet. As he rocked, he admired the photograph Stephanie had given him on his last birthday. She'd bought the thing at a high-priced photo gallery in Carmel. The photographer's name was Michael Kenna, and John knew how much Steph had paid for it. Too damn much. But she liked to support his interest in art.

In the photograph was a swing set. Steph was ever the childhood steward. The thing was apparently taken in a park somewhere in the Catskill Mountains. The whole picture was backlit by a bright street lamp. Or so John assumed. It was difficult to tell just what the source of the light was. In the foreground stood the swing set. Behind the swings were a lawn chair and a teeter-totter. These things stood framed by large willow trees which hung slack branches down in front of the light and gave the picture a sense of decline. John found himself being pulled into the photo just as he had been by the triptych. Only now, he began to guess at a meaning. Did the still photo mean to capture mechanisms of motion in an inert state? Did it want to comment on urban decay? Did it say something about childhood?

A stirring. Something deep. Like from *Die Walküre.*

In an instant the photo became a playground for the spirits of dead children, their weightless forms too light to cause the swings to move, the teeter-totter to sway. The playthings without the animation of the children were sinister. John found himself wondering what kind of man this photographer was.

Then his eyes unfocused. He had stopped rocking, and his heart hurt in his chest. His eyes teared, and he rubbed them savagely. When the clarity returned John saw the photo as it had been taken. In black and white. He stood up from his chair and approached the picture cautiously. He realized as he drew nearer that the image was grainy and nearly blurred. But it was fraught with unrealized joy. In the shadowy light of the lamp, in the semi-tones of light and dark, the swings were dead. They were not merely cold steel, they were untouched steel. The picture did not posses latent motion. The things seemed forever motionless without the help of a still photo camera.

John stepped back. His eyes hurt and his mouth was dry. He turned to grab his glass of water and in his haste poured the water all over his face. Into his eyes. He coughed and looked around the room, unsure why he felt panic. The light streaked and starred in his eyes. He paused to look longer at the light through these watery eyes, and turned his head only briefly when he thought he heard the cry of a grebe as it might sound rising off a lake.

* * *

You place the half-used roll of duct tape on the dock. Next to it you place several pounds of soldering iron. The short lengths of rod jangle like bad chimes as they roll against one another and settle on the worn boards.

Your child lies still. He's not fussing, even though he looks cold. That's a hell of a thing. You think you'll hate yourself more because of it.

But another mouth to feed. A mouth that comes with godawful expenses. Medical kinds. Not the boy's fault. But not something you can bear. Not and keep the other mouths fed. Not and keep your land. Not and keep your wife from lashing you more than she already does.

Shitty excuses. A man shouldn't have excuses. A man should find a way.

But you have. A hard way. Maybe an irredeemable way. But a way.

And just maybe there's a touch of grace in it for your boy, too, if what the doctors say is true. You don't mind going to hell if it helps your own. You're not even sure of hell. Or God, come to that.

If He's up there, He sure left you swinging in the wind.

You look down at your boy again. He's staring up, patient-like. And in that moment you see yourself from his eyes. You see your face. Hollow. Scruffy. Like a goddamned ghost.

Like you are God-damned.

You rip a length of tape and pick up the soldering iron, and—

—Daddy puts something heavy and cold against your leg. It feels like a stick. Lots of them. Except like metal. You keep still.

Then Daddy gets more tape and wraps it around your leg some more. The cold metal sticks are now tied to you real tight. You can't move your leg at all. They're so heavy.

Maybe this is a doctor thing. Maybe it's supposed to help. You like that idea. Out in the trees and by the water, this is a new way to help your sickness.

It's uncomfortable. But Mommy gets angry when you cry too much. And you've learned to be quiet and still. And you like doing that for Daddy. Especially when he looks so much in pain. You know he works very hard all the time. He always smells like work. And he's always dirty from work. This is a small thing you can do to help.

And Daddy's trying to help you. All these things are why you love him.

Daddy's eyes have tears now.

Daddy picks you up and shuffles to the edge of the dock.

The rain had started to fall hard by the time John hit I-15 north. It was quarter to three a.m. and the interstate was deserted. Those same orange halogen lamps cast down their vapid light and John fixed his mind on a vision of sunrise as he raced down the Sixth Street off-ramp. He disregarded the stoplights and came to a skidding halt four blocks later in front of the Henry Fellows Art Museum.

He grabbed his safety flashlight and jumped from the truck on a dead run for the doors. Inside the lights were off except for a few dim security lamps. *Please, God, let Kenny be working tonight,* he pleaded silently. The rain soaked his sweatshirt and Levi's even before he got to the doors. He brushed at his brows to keep it out of his eyes.

"Ken, open up, please, c'mon, open up, it's me, John." John slammed the door with his fists. The double-paned glass thudded mutely back at him.

The rain streaked down the surface in front of him, but there was no movement within.

"Ken," kicking now. "Open up, goddamnit, I need to get in, please."

Nothing moved. The rain fell in large, hard drops.

John tried to scream again, his voice giving out as he yelled for Ken to come to the door. He resorted to just kicking and hammering with his fist. Still no one came. He slid down the door to his knees and began to cry, the rain erasing the runnels of his tears as quickly as they came. There was the smell of wet pavement beneath him and the smell of wet leaves from the trees that lined the streets. The streets themselves were so flooded that the rain striking the road caused millions of small white explosions as they hit the surface.

"John?"

John looked up. Ken's head was poking out the door to his left.

"John, is that you? God, what are you doing here at this time of night? What are you doing out in the rain? Get your ass in here."

John stood, grasping the flashlight as he did. He moved past Ken evading a barrage of questions, rushing for the corner of the museum. He slipped twice on the tiles with his wet shoes and cracked his knee and elbow. But each time he fell he stood up fast and began to run again, heedless of the

162

pain. The museum was dark, just as it had been the other time Ken had arranged the midnight showing for him and Kyle. A few lamps way up on the ceiling gave enough light to walk by, but not enough to admire the paintings by.

Remnants of wine floated in the air. The hall reverberated with the squeaks of John's wet athletic shoes as he raced toward the triptych. He could hear Ken trying to catch up.

As John approached, he slowed to a walk, then took slow, careful steps. His heart was loud in his ears. He concentrated on the corner. The corner was very dark, but John knew it was there. He stopped a few feet from it and turned on the flashlight. Slowly, he brought it up toward the left panel.

The round glow of light showed first a street and a beggar on his knees. John had misjudged the placement, he swept to the left and saw a small pair of feet in the outer ring of the beam cast by the flashlight. He froze there, hearing the footfalls of his heavyset friend as he ran towards him. John blinked back a bead of sweat and lifted the light.

Wagner. Götterdämmerung. Low and painful.

The small figure's eyes were painted black.

John fell to a sitting position on the floor. But only for a moment. He quickly spied a pool of light thrown by one of the overhead security lamps, and began to crawl toward it. He'd gained the spot when Ken finally caught up to him.

"What the hell—" Ken started, but let off when he saw John hunched against the wall, crying.

"His eyes, Ken. Did you see them?" John shook with sobs. He held the flashlight against his cheek with one hand, his other hand locked under his armpit.

His own cries resonated in the large hall. They lifted up to the ceiling with its security lights. *Like a loon's.* Outside, the rain struck heavily against the windows. John shut his eyes and saw a fixed bright circle on the inside of his lids.

He had to go. Had to watch it again. Sunrise. With the old man.

It would take him about forty minutes to get there. Forty minutes if he just drove I-80 East and took the Wanship exit.

It took an hour. The rain still fell heavily, so John drove slowly. He noticed the way his truck headlamps carved swaths out of the fabric of night-time. You could see it, almost feel it, when it was raining this thick.

The rain had made the road muddy and hard to negotiate, but the sky was now clear. John got out into the mud to lock in his hubs as the sky gently passed into lighter hues. The stars gradually winked out in deference to the *old disk*. And he got to his spot.

He shut off his engine and sat in his cab, fearing—for the first time—the break of dawn. This morning he didn't play his radio. He listened only to the tick from his cooling V8 big-block.

Will the old man show up this morning? John wondered. Or, after all, was the man just a dream? After everything, would John just drive home and have sex with Marie and show up to work with a great story for Kyle? What the hell would he tell Kenny?

The rim of the mountain grew a shade brighter. Goose flesh erupted on John's skin. "What the hell am I doing?" he asked himself, incredulous. The words sounded thin in the tight space of the truck's cab.

He suddenly knew then the old guy would come. He knew it as sure as anything. "I've got to get the hell out of here." John didn't want to be around when he showed. The look of that face, those eyes in this morning light, the deep folds of skin around them... it would be too much.

The beauty of sunrise—*things will look better in the morning*—disappeared. The world wasn't going to be renewed this morning, or any morning. There would only be an old man in what looked like a gunny sack, staring toward the sun.

John imagined the look of maggots in the old guy's teeth where he finally collapsed from his hunched stance. His leathery skin cracked by the sun he so adored. The white puffs of hair torn free of their pores by gusts of wind. Drying eyelids, hardened against their blink to expose gutted sockets. The scrapes of coyote teeth along exposed lengths of bone. That was the secret to the turn of days.

John keyed the transmission and reached to put it into drive. As he did, he spied the old guy out the passenger window. The man was walking toward him. And John would swear forever that he was looking directly into his eyes.

John shook with fear. The man had a menace to him now. He moved a little more easily. His back a little straighter, his gaze steady and mean beneath white knitted brows. John cranked on the gear shift, trying to drop it into second, but the engine only raced as John began gunning the pedal.

The old guy was getting closer. The air grew colder. *Like chill air on a naked child.* John had a wild notion that if he could survive until the sun rose he would be okay. The rough revolutions of the drive shaft filled the morning with noise. John couldn't look away from the eyes which held his own. Then, as the man reached the door, John found a gear. The truck caught, hitched, and died. The old man smiled and put fingers around the door handle.

"Care if I join you, Johnny? The old disk, you know." The man climbed in, never looking away from him.

"What do you want? I haven't got anything you want. Goddamnit, leave me alone!" John was screaming, his words ringing in the confined space. His fear and confusion raising tears to his eyes.

The old man looked at him steadily. "Johnny, it's me that's got something *you* want. Something you *need.*"

John took a long, shuddering breath. "What?"

"Why do you come here, Johnny? Why do you come to watch the sun rise?" The man's voice was sure, the way a teacher's voice is when it asks a question to which it knows the answer.

The sky drew itself a shade lighter.

"I used to think it was true. I used to think it was beautiful, that things could start over again..."

"No, Johnny. I've known you for a long time." He stopped, caught John's eyes. "Since childhood. Your childhood."

John's head began to pound. *Since childhood.* John didn't know this man. He hadn't seen him before.

"Remember, Johnny. Remember a lake, a lake in the mountains not far from your boyhood home, then. You—"

John's mind slipped. He was sliding back into that dream. He wanted to thrash and scream and will it away. But low and dark and resonant, like a dark chord from *The Ring...*

* * *

You watch from the reeds as the man moves to the very end of the dock. Right above the tires nailed there as boat bumpers. You watch as he stares a long time at the child he holds in his arms. You watch as the young one's leg hangs down a bit, something taped to it.

A grebe calls from the other side of the lake, where the sun now lights the surface of the water. You don't like the sound of it. Lonely and haunting.

And now you completely understand what the man is going to do. You look at the fishing pole still in your hand, wondering if it's any kind of weapon. Wondering if you can stop this.

Your chest aches. You want to run away. You want to help.

But you also don't want to die. You don't want anything taped to your own leg. You don't want to be taken to the end of the dock. So you pray. Momma taught you about it once. You kinda figure God don't listen to one-time prayers. But you pray anyway. For the kid. You pray for the man. And you pray for yourself.

Because in this aching moment, you're not just seeing the man from your spot in the reeds. You're seeing him from the eyes of the child just as—

—You start to lower your little one toward the water. You know it will be cold on his skin. You know he will cry out. You can't go slow then. You can't take it back, either, once it's done.

You're crying. Silent crying. For your boy. For yourself. That you could do this at all. What it says about you. Your own pa would have whipped you for even thinking it.

The dock bobs a bit with your weight extended over its end. The musky smell of the lake fills your nose.

Your boy tries another smile at you. Your heart breaks. Not fanciful breaking. The actual kind. You won't be the same. You're already not the same. You are God-damned.

And there are witnesses. Your child himself. And the boy on the bank nearby. But you're all trapped in this thing now. Together. It's a different kind of witnessing. Not for the law. But for whatever lives inside. Whatever it is that condemns your heart. Forever.

Condemns all of you, except for your boy—

* * *

You smile one last time at Daddy. You can see him from close and far. You can also see yourself as if you are Daddy. And it's confusing. But mostly you are afraid now. Afraid for Daddy, too. He looks like Grampa when they said his car hit that other momma and her two little girls after he was at his favorite watering hole.

Grampa and his long gun disappeared. But before that, he always had the same face as Daddy has now.

And the only thing you've ever been able to do is try to show Daddy there were other faces to have.

But your smile doesn't work today. And you begin to shiver. You can see Daddy lowering you to the water like when he gives you a bath. Except this is not the sink. This is the lake. And there isn't any soap.

And your leg is heavy. You can't move it at all.

But that's okay. You trust Daddy, as he lowers you into the water.

You cry out. It's like icicles.

Then Daddy lets go. He's never done that before at baths.

You slip beneath the water. Your eyes seem teary. Just like Daddy's are, since you are also seeing yourself from the dock sink down. Down.

The sunshine comes on the surface above you. You see streaks of light. You see it like a bright disk above, shimmering.

You are still able to see Daddy's face a little. He's still watching over you. You're okay. But Daddy's face is getting far away. You don't think you can reach him. Your leg is taking you down. Down.

Then you take a breath. And water comes into your mouth. And you begin to shake your arms and leg.

The light is fading. The dark is getting bigger.

Daddy put you down here.

Did you do something wrong?

This isn't a bath.

You are going away from Daddy.

And then Daddy's face is gone.

And your chest and tummy heave. Cold. Hurting.

The sun is gone.

You try a cry. But it's nothing.

And a new feeling comes into your heart.

This is dying.

And you feel so bad that Daddy felt he had to kill you—

You look at the last bubbles break on the waters surface, lit like rings of gold in the sun of daybreak. If you were really a man, you'd follow the boy down. Kill yourself. But you are a coward. A God-damned one.

You will never get these images out of your head. Your eyes—

You watch the man's body heave with sobs. The boy is far down in the lake now. Drowned. You can't believe what you saw. All of it.

The air isn't just chill with morning. It's thick with confusion. Self-hatred. And fear.

You drop your fishing pole. It's seems like a stupid thing now.

You look at the man. At the water grown glassy smooth again. And the sun shining a path across it.

You raise your eyes to the sun. Another day. A new day.

John looks up into the same face, one changed by the slow march of time.

"The sun won't burn the image away, Johnny. I've tried."

John's mind was spinning. He sat in the cab of his truck, smelling oil rags and the steel of wrenches that lay beneath his seat. The light of the sun had broken on the hill top behind them, and was moving down toward the truck. *If I can only make it to sunrise,* John thought, *something will happen if I can just stall this off until then.*

"The triptych?" John asked.

The old man gave a weak smile. "No real mystery, Johnny, I told you I paint."

"You're blind," John said flatly.

The old man laughed. "What makes you think you need to see to paint?"

"And you knew I'd see it?" John stared into the eyes of the other.

"I've always been close, Johnny. Followed close." He nodded. "We got pulled into something together that morning. You've just lost some of it."

"And you've come to remind me." John's anger lit down deep. "Next you'll tell me that you were justified. What is it? Because you were poor? Because you couldn't care for the boy? Because of your goddamn wife? I should—"

"Why do you come to watch the sunrise, Johnny?" The old man looked back at the mountain ahead of them. He couldn't see it. There was no way he could see it. But he looked, anyway.

After a long moment, John let out an unintelligible cry, suddenly seeing sunrise disappear as if sinking into a cold dark lake.

"I watched you lower me into the water... as if I were your son." His eyes had filled with wet and cold that morning. He'd struggled to see beyond it. To see the light.

John now shut his eyes. Where the sun had left retinal burn, he saw only the face of the man as John descended from the surface.

When he opened his eyes again, the sky had became a shade lighter still.

"Ayuh. You can't erase the memory, because you *are* the memory."

"What the hell does that mean?" John shouted.

The old man slumped and sniffed once, his eyes glassy with tears. "Johnny, the soul of my boy... somehow... became part of you that day." His voice fell to a whisper. "Part of *us*."

"Why?" John spoke through numb lips.

"You know what, Johnny? I've lived. But only, I think, in the few moments each day when the sun draws up. When things first throw their shadows. When lake fogs begin to lift. For all the sentiment, in that brief time when the old disk floats up, I don't feel a need for forgiveness. The only important thing is the sun. The only important thing is for me to watch it rise."

John grew angry again. "Goddamnit, you tell me why!"

The old man hooked a finger around the fly window lock and bowed his head slightly.

"I don't know why, Johnny. Maybe being witness to something so frightful, you bought a share of it. I saw you that day, too. I knew you'd seen what I done. But I also knew you'd never tell it to anyone. Maybe because you didn't want to believe it. But I saw something else as you grew up, past that morning on the lake. Part of you got on with the business of life." He turned and stared at John and through him. "But part of you hasn't. Like I haven't."

John wanted to run, but his legs felt weak.

"I've dropped in on you from time to time—always without you knowing, of course. I remember when you were eleven, how you'd sit in the cellar out behind your folks' place on a bright Saturday morning, then rush up the cellar steps into the sunny afternoon, squinting and crying out with glee. Over and over you did that. That's maybe the hardest thing I ever watched you do. That's the part of you that hasn't moved on. That's the soul of the child who went down in the lake. You've got to let it go, John."

John looked toward the dawn, very close now, while in a quiet tone the old man said, "You're trying to keep seeing the light for him, Johnny. But my boy can't see no more. He's gone. Down to the bottom of the lake. We have to let him go now."

John heard none of this and watched closely as dawn prepared itself.

"John, don't watch it." The old man reached for John. His hand caught in the first rays of daybreak.

John knew now why he'd always been so glad to see clearly the slow rise of the fiery star. Why the interplay of light and shadow haunted and fright-ened him. Why the laughter of a child, or the stillness of a swing made him tremble. He would always be the child descending from the light, living and dying forever.

"There's a touch of the eternal there." John's eyes held the light. He saw nothing else.

HEALTH AND WELLNESS

Dan Wells

We are so hungry.

A man gets up from his bed; it's a small apartment in Manhattan—one kitchen, one bathroom, and one bedroom shared between two roommates. The walls are hung with posters of women and motorcycles, and the floor and table are littered with old food wrappers, cans of soda pop and beer, and some undetermined number of computers in various states of disassembly. Maybe they're radios. We recognize their basic function, but their specific purpose eludes us. Perhaps when they're put back together.

The man stumbles to the bathroom and pulls on a string, turning on a lightbulb that hangs uncovered from the center of the ceiling. "I had the most wonderful dream," says the man. The other man, still in his bed, puts his arm across his eyes to block the light, and says nothing. "I was back in Lahore," says the man in the bathroom. He grips the edges of the sink and stares into the mirror, as if he can see the images in front of him. "I was with that girl, the one from UET that I used to have a crush on. Do you remember her?"

"Shut up, Arjun," says the man in bed. "It's five o'clock in the morning."

"Kalindee," says Arjun. "She was wearing a blue sari, with gold trim and red birds that seemed to peek out of the folds of the fabric. One here, one here, and one here." He touches his chest with his finger. "I remember them perfectly. And then she looked at me and she laughed, a happy laugh, like we were old friends, and she took my hand and her skin was soft and smooth as cream."

"Kalindee talked to you *once*," said the man in bed, "in her entire life." He smiles, his wide mouth visible beside the arm that still covers his eyes. "She called you a fool and asked if you were following her."

"We were married, Muhammad," says the man in the bathroom. He pulls on the edge of the mirror and it opens, revealing a medicine cabinet sparsely filled with band-aids and painkillers and battered cans of shaving cream. "We lived in a small house, in a... damn it, why do dreams fade so quickly?" He takes a plastic box from the shelf, the edges rounded like a giant lozenge. "A small house in... well, in Lahore, somewhere by UET, in our same old neighborhood I think, because I recognized the streets, but it was a house, not an apartment." He frowns. "I think it was a house."

"Get to the good part before you forget it," says Muhammad. "Was she good in bed?"

Arjun whirls to yell at him, brandishing the plastic box like a weapon, but as he shouts the first angry syllable the box flies from his hand, hits the wall with an audible crack, and then bounces off the sink on its way to the floor. "Damn it," he says again.

"What was that?" asks Muhammad, sitting up in his bed.

"I dropped my dispenser," says Arjun, kneeling to pick it up. "It's cracked."

"I didn't hear a hundred vitamins raining out onto the floor," says Muhammad, laying back down. "It's fine."

"It still opens," says Arjun, flipping up the lid with a tiny, plastic click. He pulls out two vitamins, pauses, and frowns. "What were we talking about?"

"Your dream," said Muhammad, closing his eyes. "You were banging Kalindee Chopra."

Arjun hesitates, staring at the vitamins. "It wasn't like that, it was... I don't remember. Why can you never remember the good dreams?"

"No one remembers any dreams," says Muhammad. "Now shut up so I can get back to mine."

Arjun puts the vitamins in his mouth and swallows. "Dream about Kalindee," he says to Muhammad, "and I'll throw you out the window."

We watch, and we wait.

"I don't know why you even take those things," says another man. They're at work, wearing white shirts and black ties in a maze of beige cubicles. The new man is sitting backward on a rolling desk chair, watching Arjun as he sorts through a pile of electronic components. It looks similar to the pile Arjun has at home: more expensive, perhaps, but just as chaotic. Puru leans forward, eyes eager, voice animated, his hands drawing invisible patterns in the air. "The Health and Wellness Supplement Initiative: free pills from the United States government. That's the first scene of every dystopian novel every written."

"They're vitamins, Puru," says Arjun. "Not... Prozac."

Puru shakes his head. "And you're so sure of that? Mr. Rangan, from the market on 27th Street, says he can barely sleep anymore since he started taking them."

"He's healthier," says Arjun. "He has more energy now. And he's definitely not using all that extra energy just standing behind the counter all day, so it's still there at night."

"He *sits* behind the counter," says Puru, "but that's not the point."

"Well there you go," says Arjun, as if that explains everything. He bends low over his materials, plugging one piece into another and looking at the monitor beside him. Whatever he sees there displeases him, and he takes the pieces apart again.

"You're missing the big picture," says Puru. "Your precious little vitamins are more than just vitamins—they have to be. They've got amphetamines in them, or caffeine, or something. Why would the government give a bunch of poor people vitamins?"

"To make us healthier?" offers Arjun. "Is that really so impossible?"

"This is the U.S. government we're talking about," says Puru. "They're not in the business of baseless philanthropy—just making people happy for no good reason. They want power, and power means control, and control means they give everyone free pills full of uppers and downers and whatever else they can cram in there."

"Uppers *and* downers?"

"I'm not a biochemist," says Puru. "I don't know how they do it. But they do it, I guarantee: whatever it takes to keep you hard-working and compliant —they want to control you, but they want you to be worth controlling, too, because otherwise what's the point? Which is why there's also vitamins and minerals and probably antibiotics in there, too. Keep you healthy."

"I thought you said they weren't vitamins."

"I said they weren't *just* vitamins," says Puru. "Obviously they're *at least* vitamins, or the lie would be too easy to catch."

"Occam's Razor," says Arjun, looking up from his work. "The government provides health care to everyone, regardless of income or citizenship: if you've got a green card, you get medicine. But medicine is expensive, and they've crunched the same numbers everyone else has, and they know that it's cheaper to keep us healthy in the first place than to try to fix us when we're sick. So: free vitamins."

"Well, obviously," says Puru. "But that's just Plan A. Once you go to all that trouble of making vitamins and distributing them to the poor, why would you *not* put some form of populace control in them? They'd be stupid not to. And every three months, when you pick up a new dose and a new dispenser, they check a box in their secret file that says, 'Arjun Gupta is a good little immigrant, who takes his pills on time.'"

"Why would they wait three months?" asks Arjun, though the look on his face is more derisive than sincere. "Why not keep tabs on you every day, through secret cameras and monitoring devices?" He shakes his head and goes back to his work. "If you're going to spin conspiracy theories, Puru, at least have the decency to go full Paranoid Wacko."

"You think you're joking," says Puru, "but what else are the dispensers for? Why not just give you a bottle of pills like a regular pharmacy? Before it broke, your box was spying on you."

We can tell that Puru has thought about this a lot. We will keep watching.

Six nights later Arjun is glowing, but we are the only ones who see it. His roommate Muhammad does not, and neither do the women. They sit on Arjun's couch, young and pretty, dressed more finely than the small apartment is accustomed to. The men have cleaned up their pizza boxes and kebab wrappers, and flipped over their posters—each one is mounted on cardboard, with a Bollywood actress on one side and a travel photo on the other. Tonight only the travel photos are displayed. The electronics still cover the table, because where else can they go?

"I remember the entire thing," says Arjun. "It was crazy. I was in my office, only it was also my home. You know how things in dreams can get mixed up inside each other? It was my office, and my home, at the same time."

"You spend too much time in your office," says one of the women, smiling as she teases him. We think she likes him, but that's not why we're here. We are hungry.

"I had two kitchens," says Arjun. "One of them was a food court, like in a mall, but right next to a conference room."

"Maybe you spend too much time in the mall," says the other woman, and both women laugh, showing their proud white teeth, and glancing sidelong at the men to make sure they are watching.

"The second kitchen was a fake," says Arjun, "like a set from an infomercial. That was my job: demonstrating an orange juice machine, and selling it to the audience. I didn't even see the machine, I just knew that's what was going on, the way you know things in dreams."

"I think the biggest place you're spending too much time," says Muhammad, "is in your dreams."

The women laugh again, good-natured and fun. "I can never remember my dreams," says the one who likes Arjun. "Last night I was... in an orchestra? I think? I don't know why, I can't play any instruments. Maybe I could in my dream, but I don't remember."

"But that's the thing, Bina," says Arjun. "I remember everything. All week, now: I can remember ever detail of every dream I've had the past six nights. Two nights ago I went sailing, searching for buried treasure at the coordinates 7245832."

"That's not a real coordinate," says Bina. "Don't you need two numbers to find something? Like the x and y on a graph."

"Of course," says Arjun. "I'm sure it's just something my brain made up, some random string of numbers from my subconscious. But I remember it: 7245832. How can I remember that? I can barely remember what I had for lunch three days ago, but my dreams are all there, as clear as... movies in my mind."

"You're obsessed," says Muhammad. We didn't notice when he did it, but somehow he has his arm around the other woman now, resting on the back of the couch just above her shoulders.

"I wish I could remember my dreams," says the other woman. "Sometimes

I can fly—I'd love to remember that. There's a feeling to it, kind of like exhilaration but also kind of, just... familiar. Like, 'Of course you fly,' just jump and don't come back down. Like you've always been able to do it."

"I get that, too," says Bina. She closes her eyes, as if she's trying to recall the exact sense of weightlessness, of ability, of *rightness* she feels in her dreams. It is hard for us to watch this, but how can we stop? They will keep telling the stories, and we will keep listening until we starve.

"I think it's the vitamins," says Arjun. He hesitates as he speaks, as if he still can't decide whether he should say the words out loud. "The free ones, from the government. I know Muhammad takes them. Do you take them, Bina?"

"Of course," Bina says. "Everyone does."

"And you still can't remember your dreams?" asks Arjun.

"I told you he's obsessed," says Muhammad. "It's all he ever talks about."

Arjun looks at the other woman. "Suravi, do you take the vitamins?"

"Why wouldn't I?" the other woman asks, and frowns. "You're not one of those conspiracy nuts, are you?"

"No, no," says Arjun, waving his hands in front him like he's erasing a drawing in the sand. "I mean, I take them, too; I don't think they're bad. But I wondered if maybe this was a side effect: that you could remember your dreams. Have you heard of anyone else like that?"

"This is turning into the most boring date ever," says Muhammad. The women smile politely. "Who wants a drink?"

Muhammad stands up, stepping to the counter and sink that serves as their kitchen. Suravi follows, helping him with the glasses and the ice. Bina sits on the couch and looks at Arjun, cocking her head to the side as she watches him. He doesn't seem to notice her. After a moment she brushes his knee with her fingertips, just barely, and says him name softly.

"Arjun?"

"Bina," he says, his eyes focusing on her. "Yes. Sorry. I was just daydreaming."

"It's not the pills," says Arjun. "It's the dispenser. It's the only thing that makes sense."

Another week has passed, and he still remembers every second of every dream. They fill his mind like a cloud of light, spilling out through his eyes and shining from his ears and pouring from his mouth and nose like smoke from an incense burner. He can't see the light, but he can see its effects, the words and people and places from his dreams flashing in the corners of his vision.

"Just stop taking the pills, already," says Muhammad. His careless attitude is gone; he is worried about his friend.

"I stopped three days ago," says Arjun. "The dreams still come—and it's not just the dreams, it's the nightmares, too. Last night I was chased by a dog, one of the mangy grey ones that used to roam the streets in India, but way bigger than it should have been. I couldn't run; it was like my legs were in syrup, and every step was an effort, and the dog was slow but it caught up with me, step by step, and I couldn't get away and I couldn't wake up and it tore me apart, snapping me up in its teeth and shaking me like a doll, chewing me and swallowing me and I remember *every damn second of it*." He leans forward, his gaunt eyes pleading from within their dark, sleepless circles, his hands shaking as he holds the dispenser. "Do you realize what that's like? Do you have any idea?"

"We need to get you to a doctor," says Muhammad. "Those pills have messed you up—"

"It's not the pills!" Arjun shouts. "Thousands of people take the vitamins, tens of thousands, and all of them are fine, but how many broke their dispenser? I'm the only one. I broke it and it's hurting me."

"You're paranoid," says Muhammad."Not like Puru—you're mentally ill. I don't know if it's a psychotic break, or you're too stressed at work, or maybe you're reacting to the pills, but you've got to let me take you to the doctor—"

He puts his hand on Arjun's arm, but Arjun throws him off, clutching the dispenser. "Don't touch me!" His swinging arm sweeps the table, and piles of electronics clatter to the floor. Arjun hugs the dispenser to his chest, curling in on himself like a caterpillar, cocooning himself in his own arms. Muhammad steps back, staring at him, wondering what to do, then grabs his jacket and walks to the door.

"I'm going to get a doctor," says Muhammad. "If you won't go to one, I'll find one who'll come to you." He pauses at the door, thinking, then grabs Arjun's keys and wallet from the counter. "Stay here. Don't do anything stupid." He closes the door and locks it tightly behind him. We listen with Arjun as Muhammad's footsteps fade into the distance.

"It's the dispenser," says Arjun, unfurling himself to look at it again. "Why give them to us if they don't do anything? They have to do something, and mine's doing it wrong. All I have to do is..." He examines the crack in the plastic shell, and picks up a screwdriver from his workspace. The tip is too thick to fit into the crack, so he sets it down and goes to the kitchen counter, rifling through the drawers for a knife. He finds one, a long chopping knife, much bigger than he needs but with a thin, sharp blade. He slides it into the crack, careful not to push too deep, and twists it, levering the plastic shell until it starts to bend and then break, the crack widening, the dispenser splitting open like a melon. He peers inside, sees the three-month pill supply, half-gone now, nestled in a plastic bag like eggs in a sack; sees the brick of electronics, the circuits and wires and processors and some bits he's never seen before.

A small, red light is blinking, and then it stops.

Arjun studies the electronics, clearing a space on his table and sitting down to his tools. "This is the battery," he says, tapping it with a pair of tweezers. He moves them to a small black square. "This is the chip that runs it. And this..." He taps the tweezers on the center of the device, where a wide metal circle connects to the circuits with short blue wires. "Not a magnet, but similar. A sensor, maybe? And what's behind it?" The circuit board is clipped into a set of plastic hooks, and he pops them open and pulls it out. The back side of the device, what would be the top when the dispenser is sitting upright, is a long, metal coil, like a copper spring, but only connected on one end. We don't know what it is, but Arjun has studied electrical engineering at one of India's finest schools. He works as a technician, and even in his spare time he plays with machines. He recognizes the coil instantly, and by his sharp intake of breath we can tell he doesn't like it. "That's an antenna," he whispers, lowering his voice as if someone is suddenly listening. "It's transmitting. They really *are* spying on us."

And then a surge of dream rolls out like a cloud, enveloping him, and he looks up and talks to it, seeing a person who isn't there.

"Kalindee," he says. "They're spying on us, just like I told you before. Find the children, quickly—we have to go, now, before they can find us—"

And then the doorbell rings, and Arjun knows that Kalindee is a dream, but the doorbell could be anything. The dreams are everywhere for him now: the other side of the door might hold Muhammad and a doctor, it might hold a government agent, it might hold a big black dog with yellow eyes and dripping jowls. Arjun doesn't move. The knock sounds again. Arjun creeps forward, muttering to himself.

"If it's just a dream it can't hurt me," he says. "If it's just a dream maybe the dispenser is a dream. I can't tell the difference anymore. Maybe I cracked open the dispenser and there was nothing inside, just vitamins, and I made the rest up. Maybe everything will be okay." He puts his hand on the door-knob and pauses. The visitor knocks a third time. Arjun opens the door.

"Good morning!" The voice is bright and chipper. A young man stands in the hallway, clean-shaven, white, a toolbox in his hand. He wears a plain blue jumpsuit. On his left breast is a nametag: Jim. "I'm Jim!" says Jim. "Are you Mr. Arjun Gupta?"

"Yes," says Arjun, confused. "Who are you?"

"I'm a service technician from the clinic," says Jim cheerfully. "We got an alert that your vitamin dispenser was broken; I'm here to offer you a replacement."

"It's transmitting," Arjun accuses.

"How else could we come help you when it's broken?" asks Jim. "Mind if I come in?" There's room to squeeze through, and he does, without waiting for Arjun's approval. He sees the mess on the table and whistles. "Looks like everything broke, am I right?" Arjun stammers, and Jim laughs. "Just kidding. You do this for a living, right? Electrical engineering?"

"How do you—?"

"We're spying on you," says Jim, and laughs again, slapping Arjun lightly on the shoulder. "I'm just playing, buddy." He holds up the work order in his hand. "You told us about your job when you signed up for the vitamins. Now." He looks back at the table, identifying the broken pieces of the old dispenser and scooping them up. "Looks like this shattered pretty good. Did you pry it open yourself? These things are more solid than you think—takes more than a drop on the floor to crack the shell. Impact-resistant plastic."

"But that's exactly what happened," says Arjun. "It slipped out of my hands two weeks ago—"

"Whoa," says Jim, spinning around. The look on his face is suddenly serious. "You're saying this broke two weeks ago?"

"Yes, it slipped out of my hands—"

"We didn't get the alert until ten *minutes* ago," says Jim, peering at the dispenser more closely. "Is it faulty?"

"Ten minutes ago is when I opened it," says Arjun. "Two weeks ago is when it broke." He points. "The side of it cracked, right there." He hesitates a moment, not wanting to look crazy, not wanting to *be* crazy, and when he speaks his voice is careful, probing. "It's the dispenser that does it, right? The dreams? I can't forget them anymore. Even when I'm awake they're everywhere, like flies buzzing through my mind."

Jim doesn't move, looking toward the dispenser but not at it. "Dreams?"

"That's a transmitter," says Arjun, "but it's more than just a service alarm. That processor is too big. You're reading data, and you're sending it somewhere." He swallows. "What have you done to us?"

Jim sighs, and speaks into the cuff of his jumpsuit. "He knows. Prep the van."

"What?" asks Arjun, stepping back, but it's too late, and when Jim turns around he already has a syringe in his hand, and he sticks it into Arjun's neck with practiced expertise, sedating him and catching him in a single movement. Arjun loses consciousness immediately, and already the dreams are swirling around him, surging and growing, and even when Jim pulls a bag over Arjun's head we can still see the glow like a dark, pulsing heart.

"Mr. Gupta."

Arjun stirs.

"Mr. Gupta."

Arjun opens his eyes, then squeezes them shut at the brightness in the bare, white room. He's handcuffed to a chair, seated at an empty table. A man in a suit with a thick, graying beard sits across from him. Jim stands in the corner, arms folded, waiting.

We are waiting too. It's almost time.

"Mr. Gupta," says the man with the beard, and this time Arjun is able to keep his eyes open. "Good," says the man, and he smiles, though not out of kindness. "My name is Jim Holder."

"Jim?" asks Arjun.

"It's a common name," says Holder. "Just call me Holder. My official title is Chief Liaison In Charge, which is a silly way of saying that I lead a project for the NSA. In this case, Project Horn, which you know as the Health and Wellness Supplement Initiative. The vitamins."

"The vitamins come from the NSA?" asks Arjun.

"I said the NSA is overseeing the project," says Holder, shaking his head. "The vitamins, and myself, for that matter, come from another government organization called NARPA. It's like DARPA, but instead of defense we focus on 'non-categorized research.'"

"What does that mean?" asks Arjun, though he does not expect a response.

"The supernatural," says Holder. He says it like it were the most normal thing in the world. "The simplest way to put it is that we use the paranormal for our own ends, just like we do with any other resource. Most of our projects are weaponizations: turning a fire demon into a bomb, that sort of thing. Boring stuff, if you ask me—anyone can make a bomb. Downloading an entire population's subconscious, on the other hand, that's something new. And in certain rare cases, it goes wrong. I'm very sorry for any suffering you may have experienced."

Arjun stares at the man, his mouth open. Wisps of dream roil out like fog, pooling on the floor, just covering Holder's shoes. He doesn't seem to notice.

"So you *have* been spying on us," says Arjun. "All the nuts, all the conspiracy nuts, they're all right."

"Some of them are right," says Holder. "Certainly no more than probability suggests—an infinite number of conspiracy nuts on an infinite number of blog posts are bound to be right about something. But none of them have the details right. You got closer than any of them, and you still had most of the real, nitty-gritty details wrong."

"It's the dreams, right?" asks Arjun. "You're using that dispenser to read our dreams, and mine was broken and it was... messing them up somehow. Messing up my whole head."

"Not reading, but downloading," says Holder. "It turns out that dreams aren't just unconscious thoughts, they're an actual substance, or at least they are substantial. At any rate, they can be moved and collected and stored in a way that thoughts and memories can't. I don't understand all the little ins and outs, but that's the gist of it: dreams accrue in your mind during sleep, and our dispensers extract them. What the Health and Wellness Supplement Initiative does, above and beyond all the health and wellness stuff, is give the NSA direct access to the subconscious thoughts of an entire population."

"Or at least the poor, immigrant subset of that population," says Arjun.

"That's the group most likely to produce terrorists," says Holder with a shrug. "Call it profiling if you like, but it works."

"It's illegal," says Arjun.

Holder smiles as if the accusation were hilarious. "Are dreams protected by law in India? They're not here."

"It's an invasion of privacy," says Arjun. "Just because you're stealing something nobody knows you can steal doesn't make it not stealing."

"Now you sound like Puru."

Arjun's eyes widen. "Do you know everything about me?"

"Relax," says Holder, "we're not interested in you." He pulls a smartphone from his pocket and taps the screen a few times. "Puru Mukopadhaya, who sits in the cubicle next to you at work, is slightly more interesting in that he is a practicing Ahmadi Muslim."

"Is that against the law?" asks Arjun.

"If it was we'd arrest him," says Holder. "But it *does* make him a person of interest, and because he refuses to take the vitamins, we watch him through you."

"Why can't you just... plant a dispenser in his house somewhere?" asks Arjun. "Hide a transmitter in his bedside lamp, or whatever it is you used to do when all you had was hidden microphones."

"We would," says Holder, "except the dispenser is only half of the system. Supernatural things are as much a part of the ecosystem as anything natural; if dreams are a substance we can use as a resource, you can bet that some-thing out there started using it before we got to it. Have you heard of the Oneiroi?"

"Should I have?"

"Greek mythology," says Holder. "According to the legends they live in a place called Erebos, a land of eternal darkness beyond the rising sun." He waves his hand dismissively. "Typical myth-y nonsense. They used to say that these things would bring dreams, but just because some old Greek guy *observed* the Oneiroi doesn't mean he *understood* them. He figured out the connection to dreams, but he got it backward: they eat dreams. They consume them, like rats eating garbage, and just like rats and garbage it's actually a pretty beneficial service. We don't want those dreams cluttering up our heads, as you've discovered, so the Oneiroi feeding habits are a pretty big help. We have a symbiotic relationship, you could say, like those little birds that pick food out of a hippo's teeth. But since now we wanted the dreams for ourselves, we had to drive the Oneiroi away first. We studied them for a while, and eventually came up with... I guess you'd call it an inoculation. The pills we give you include—in addition to some very good vitamins—an extra ingredient that changes your psychic chemistry. You take a pill, the Oneiroi can't feed, we siphon off the dreams, everyone's happy. As long as the process works, nobody even knows we've done anything at all."

"But then my siphon broke," says Arjun.

"Your siphon broke," says Holder with a nod. "The dreams build up, and they don't have anywhere to go. This has, as you've noticed, some deleterious effects on your mental health."

The fog of dreams is up to their knees by now.

"Why are you telling me all of this?" asks Arjun. "Can you fix me? Can you give me a new siphon to drain them all away?"

"To the latter questions, yes," says Holder. "I have technicians working on that right now, matching a new dispenser to your neural patterns. It's a careful balance—that's why Muhammad's dispenser didn't siphon your dreams. They have to be precise. As to your former question: I want you to work for us."

Arjun laughs, involuntarily. "You're joking."

"Not at all," says Holder. "You're a brilliant engineer. You didn't figure out everything we're doing, but like I said earlier, you got closer than anybody ever has. We work in an industry that doesn't exist, using forces most people think are fairy tales. I can't exactly post a job opening for 'Supernatural Engineer, must have experience with electronics, data analysis, and boogeymen.' I get my talent by looking for the people who are smart enough to look for us. Once we get you up to speed, you'd be a great asset to our team."

"After what you've done to me?" asks Arjun. "I'll never work for you—I don't want anyone I know to work for you. I don't even want anyone I know to take your damn pills—"

"Now, easy there," says Holder. "I understand that you're angry, but you can't stop taking the pills."

"The hell I can't."

"Of course, eventually, but think this through." Holder is deadly serious. "The Oneiroi are ravenous, and with the Supplement Initiative there's not enough dreams to go around. We can't see it, but your head is like a beacon right now: two weeks' worth of sweet, delicious dreams, tantalizing but just out of reach. This room is probably swarming with Oneroi right now, just waiting for your pills to wear off. If you don't let us clear your head first with a new siphon, you'll start a feeding frenzy so horrific there won't be any of you left—they won't stop at the dreams, they'll eat your memories, your intelligence, your capacity for sentient thought. Even the people near you could be at risk—they're like piranhas in the water, so caught up in eating they can't distinguish food or friends or anything else. You have to... What's wrong?"

Arjun is turning pale, his eyes wide with fear. "How long?" he asks, and swallows to wet his throat. "How long does it take before the pills wear off?"

Holder looks at him fiercely. "How long ago did you stop?"

"Three days," Arjun whispers, and Holder stands up so fast his chair falls down.

"Jim, why didn't you tell me he'd stopped taking them?"

"I didn't know!" shouts Jim.

Both men are scrambling for the door now, shouting and pounding for someone to open it, but it's too late. The dreams are ready.

We gnash our astral teeth, hundreds of us in a starving madness, and with a soundless howl we swarm in to feed.

We are so hungry.

CONTRIBUTORS

Marie Brennan is an anthropologist and folklorist who shamelessly pillages her academic fields for material. She is currently misapplying her professors' hard work to the Victorian adventure series *The Memoirs of Lady Trent*; the first book of that series, *A Natural History of Dragons*, has been nominated for a World Fantasy Award. She is also the author of the doppelganger duo-logy of *Warrior and Witch*, the urban fantasy *Lies and Prophecy*, the *Onyx Court* historical fantasy series, and more than forty short stories. When she's not obsessing over historical details too minute for anybody but her to care about, she practices shorin-ryu karate and pretends to be other people in role-playing games (which sometimes find their way into her writing).

D.J. Butler is a lawyer by training and a consultant in his day job, and he's been writing speculative fiction for all audiences since 2010. His novel *City of the Saints*, a four-part gonzo action Mormon steampunk adventure tale, was a 2012 Whitney Award finalist. He also writes the *Rock Band Fights Evil* series of action-horror pulp fiction novella-length adventures, and *The Buza System* (first book *Crecheling*) of dark science fiction for young adults. His website is www.davidjohnbutler.com.

Michaelbrent Collings is a #1 bestselling novelist and produced screen-writer. As novelist, Michaelbrent is one of the most successful indie horror writers in the U.S. He has been one of Amazon's top selling horror writers for years and has written bestsellers in the horror, fantasy, thriller, sci-fi, and general fiction lists for every major electronic retailer, often outselling the likes of Stephen King and Dean Koontz. He is a bestseller in over 40 countries, and his audiobooks have spent months on Audible's sci-fi and horror bestseller lists. As a screenwriter, he is a member of the Writers Guild of America, and his scripts have been made into internationally released movies starring Eric McCormack (*Will & Grace*; *Perception*), Elizabeth Rohm (*American Hustle*), and Kaylee DeFer (*Gossip Girl*). He has optioned numerous other scripts, and has several properties currently in development. He also makes awesome chocolate-chip waffles. His website, where you can find out more about him, his books, and scads of articles on the art and craft of writing, is at michaelbrentcollings.com.

Larry Correia is the New York Times bestselling, award winning author of the *Monster Hunter International* series, the *Grimnoir Chronicles*, and the *Dead Six* military thrillers. A former accountant, machine gun dealer, and firearms instructor Larry lives in the mountains of northern Utah with his wife and children.

Steven Diamond founded and runs the review site Elitist Book Reviews (www.elitistbookreviews.com), which was nominated for the Hugo Award in 2013 & 2014. He writes for Baen, Privateer Press, and numerous small publications. *Shared Nightmares* is his first voyage into the realm of anthology editing. Steve lives in Utah with two kids and his awesome wife. He's a bit (a ton) fanatical about the New Orleans Saints and Oakland Athletics. He also thoroughly enjoys having his likeness killed off in other people's novels.

Paul Genesse visited the Kyoto imperial palace in May of 2014 and learned the entire complex burned down eight times. Three of the fires happened over a very short span of time in the late ninth century A.D., just as they occurred in the story, "Onnen." True historical events abound in "Onnen," as do many elements from traditional Japanese ghost stories. Hauntings are a subject Paul loves reading and writing about, and he frequently includes ghosts in his fiction. His first novel in the Iron Dragon series, *The Golden Cord*, which is the bestselling fantasy novel Five Star Books has ever had, features a haunted hero. The second and third books in the series, *The Dragon Hunters*, and *The Secret Empire*, feature several malicious ghosts bent on revenge. Paul has sold over a dozen short stories, which appear in various DAW anthologies, and elsewhere. He is also the editor of the five volumes in the demon-themed *Crimson Pact* shared multiverse anthology series. He worked full time as a cardiac nurse for 17 years, and now works as a clinical analyst for a healthcare company. He has also worked as a copy editor, computer game consultant, and naturally he enjoys speaking at conventions. He is a huge fan of J.R.R. Tolkien's books, and loves *The Hobbit* and *The Lord of the Rings* movies. He wants to become the nerd Jimmy Fallon and enjoys interviewing movie and TV stars at large media conventions like Salt Lake Comic Con. Friend him on Facebook, follow him on Twitter @Paul_Genesse, or explore paulgenesse.com.

Max Gladstone has been thrown from a horse in Mongolia and nominated (twice!) for the John W Campbell Best New Writer Award. Tor Books published *Full Fathom Five*, the third novel in Max's Craft Sequence (preceded by *Three Parts Dead* and *Two Serpents Rise*) in July 2014. *Last First Snow*, the next Craft Sequence novel, will hit shelves in July 2015. Max's game *Choice of the Deathless* was nominated for a 2013 XYZZY Award, and his short fiction has appeared on Tor.com and in *Uncanny Magazine*.

Sarah A. Hoyt has published two dozen novels and over a hundred short stories. Possibly her best known work is *Darkship Thieves*, winner of the Prometheus Award 2011. She was born in Portugal and lives in CO with her husband, two sons and four cats (please don't ask about the cats.) In her free time she also writes fantasy and mystery and has been known to use the pen names Sarah Marques, Sarah D'Almeida and Elise Hyatt. The story in this anthology scared her!

Author of seven novels including *The Stormcaller, Moon's Artifice* and the forthcoming *Old Man's Ghosts*, **Tom Lloyd** was born in 1979 in Berkshire. After a degree in International Relations he went straight into publishing where he still works. He never received the memo about suitable jobs for writers and consequently has never been a kitchen-hand, hospital porter, pigeon hunter, or secret agent. He lives in Oxford, isn't one of those authors who gives a damn about the history of the font used in his books and only believes in forms of exercise that allow him to hit something. Visit him on-line at www.tomlloyd.co.uk.

Peter Orullian has worked at Xbox for over a decade, which is good, be-cause he's a gamer. He's toured internationally with various bands and been a featured vocalist at major rock and metal festivals, which is good, because he's a musician. He's also learned when to hold his tongue, which is good, because he's a contrarian. Peter has published several short stories, which he thinks are good. *The Unremembered* is his first novel, which he hopes you will think is good. He lives in Seattle, where it rains all the damn time. He has nothing to say about that. Visit him at www.orullian.com.

Howard Tayler is the writer and illustrator behind *Schlock Mercenary*, the Hugo-nominated science fiction comic strip. Howard has written SF horror for the *Space Eldritch* and *Space Eldritch II: The Haunted Stars* anthologies, and he writes fantasy tie-in fiction for Privateer Press under their Skull Island X imprint. Howard co-hosts the Hugo and Parsec award-winning "Writing Excuses" podcast, a weekly 'cast for genre-fiction writers, with Mary Robinette Kowal, Brandon Sanderson, and Dan Wells. They collabo-rated together to create the *Shadows Beneath* anthology. His most recent printed work is *Schlock Mercenary: Massively* Parallel, which was on the 2010 Hugo ballot. *Schlock Mercenary* may be found online at schlock-mercenary.com. Howard lives in Orem, Utah with his wife Sandra, their four children, and one ungrateful, archetypally imperious cat.

When **Dan Wells** was 5 years old he got autographs from both Darth Vader and Mr. Rogers. He owns more than 300 board games. He has visited fif-teen different countries, and lived in three. He was diagnosed with hypo-chondria as a child, but it's mostly gone now. He memorizes poetry for fun. He will eat pretty much anything at least once. He collects ugly ties. He is terrified of needles, mediocrity, and senile dementia. When he dies, his wife has specific instructions to play Michael Jackson's "Don't Stop 'til You Get Enough" at his funeral.

If you enjoyed this book, check out some of the other publications from Cold Fusion Media:

Space Eldritch

Science fiction goes occult in *Space Eldritch*, a volume of seven original novelettes and novellas of Lovecraftian pulp space opera. Featuring work by Brad R. Torgersen (Hugo/Nebula/Campbell nominee), Howard Tayler (multiple Hugo nominee), and Michael R. Collings (author of over 100 books), plus a foreword by New York Times bestselling author Larry Correia, *Space Eldritch* inhabits the intersection between the eternal adventure of the final frontier and the inhuman darkness between the stars.

Space Eldritch II: The Haunted Stars

The cold of interstellar space is again closer than you think as eleven authors —including New York Times bestseller Larry Correia, Nebula winner Eric James Stone, Amazon #1 bestseller Michaelbrent Collings, and multiple Hugo nominee Howard Tayler—explore what happens when space opera meets Lovecraftian cosmic horror.

Arcane Sampler
Edited by Nathan Shumate

A bite-sized collection featuring twelve unsettling original stories, *Arcane Sampler* demonstrates the kind of macabre storytelling that characterizes the *Arcane* series of anthologies — for only 99 cents! Included:

- The performers in a traveling carnival suddenly find themselves in mortal danger from their latest exhibit...
- A Bible salesman discovers a reclusive family who worships something older... and closer...
- A good Samaritan stopping to give roadside assistance encounters something far more dangerous than a flat tire...

Arcane
Edited by Nathan Shumate

The first full-length anthology of this series features thirty stories by some of the freshest blood in the horror, dark fantasy and weird fiction fields! Included:

- An office worker returns from bereavement leave to find his workplace changing before his eyes...

- A priest excites his village to the greatest show of devotion to their god ever seen…
- A mortician sees all of his immaculate handiwork destroyed when his clients start rising…

Arcane II
Edited by Nathan Shumate

This second volume of the *Arcane* anthology series presents twenty-one more stories of dark imagination. Included:

- A landlord finds something left behind by a former tenant, something with a will of its own…
- A bride explores her new husband's manor house, seeking the mystery that overshadows his life…
- A survivor of the apocalypse sees an insidious change infecting the few remaining humans…

The Golden Age of Crap
by Nathan Shumate

Just because you can't respect a movie doesn't mean you can't enjoy it. *The Golden Age of Crap* serves up a sampling of junk-food flicks that gained their audiences on videocassette rental shelves during the '80s and '90s, a time when one couldn't visit the video rental store without being tempted by Italian post-apocalyptic adventures, ninja revenge yarns, and zombie-filled "camcorder epics." The movies covered here run from sleeper hits (*Phantasm II*) to cult favorites (*The Dead Next Door*), from unknown stinkers (*Plutonium Baby*) to undiscovered gems (*America's Deadliest Home Video*), all examined with a critical but fun-loving eye.

www.coldfusionmedia.us

COLD FUSION MEDIA